A NIGHT IN ANNWN

The Strange Story of Willy Jones's Near-Death Experience

by

Owen Jones

Copyright

Copyright © Owen Jones Author 2025

ISBN: 978-1-0683538-2-6

Megan Publishing Services
http://meganpublishingservices.com

All rights reserved.

Disclaimer:

This novel is a work of fiction. Names, characters, businesses, places, events, and incidents are either the product of the author's imagination or used in a fictitious manner. Any resemblance to actual persons, living or dead, or actual events is purely coincidental.

The author has made every effort to portray the characters, settings, and events in this book accurately and in a manner consistent with the storyline. However, creative liberties may have been taken for the sake of the narrative.

Readers are reminded that the characters and events depicted in this novel are entirely fictional, and any similarities to real individuals, whether living or deceased, or actual occurrences are unintentional.

The author and publisher disclaim any liability, loss, or risk incurred as a consequence, directly or indirectly, of the use and application of any contents of this novel. Any resemblance to persons, living or dead, events, or locales is entirely coincidental.

The Annwn – Heaven Series

Annwn can be seen as the ancient Welsh word for Heaven, although Annwn was underground – or even under the mountains. This led early Christian missionaries from around the Mediterranean to think that they were satanists and devil-worshippers.

1. A Night in Annwn
The Strange Story of Old Willy Jones' NDE

-

2. Life in Annwn
The Story of Willy Jones's Life in Heaven

-

3. Leaving Annwn
Returning to Earth on a Mission!

Inspirational Quotes

Believe not in anything simply because you have heard it,

Believe not in anything simply because it was spoken and rumoured by many,

Believe not in anything simply because it was found written in your religious texts,

Believe not in anything merely on the authority of teachers and elders,

Believe not in traditions because they have been handed down for generations,

But after observation and analysis, if anything agrees with reason and is conducive to the good and benefit of one and all, accept it and live up to it.

Gautama Buddha

Great Spirit, whose voice is on the wind, hear me.

Let me grow in strength and knowledge.

Make me ever behold the red and purple sunset.

May my hands respect the things you have given me.

Teach me the secrets hidden under every leaf and stone, as you have taught people for ages past.

Let me use my strength, not to be greater than my brother, but to fight my greatest enemy – myself.

Let me always come before you with clean hands and an open heart, that as my Earthly span fades like the sunset, my Spirit shall return to you without shame.

(Based on a traditional **Sioux prayer**)

"I do not seek to walk in the footsteps of the Wise People of old; I seek what they sought".
Matsuo Basho

"Have I not commanded you? Be strong and courageous. Do not be afraid; do not be discouraged, for the LORD your God will be with you wherever you go".
Joshua 1:9

"Whatever misfortune befalls you [people], it is because of what your own hands have done- God forgives much-"
Quran 42:30

Myself when young did eagerly frequent
Doctor and Saint, and heard great Argument
About it and about; but oft-times
Came out, by the same Door as in I went.
Omar Khayyam
The Rubaiyat XXIX.

Contact Details

BlueSky: owen-author.bsky.social
Facebook: AngunJones
Instagram: owen_author
LinkedIn: owencerijones
Pinterest: owen_author
TikTok: @owen_author
X: @owen_author
Blog: Megan Publishing Services

Join our newsletter for insider information on Owen Jones' books and writing by adding your email to:

http://meganpublishingservices.com/

Table of Contents

1. WILLY JONES

"Dad, are you up yet?" shouted Becky into the dingy, unlit cottage as she closed the front door behind her with a bang in case he wasn't even awake. She immediately wondered whether she should have left it open. The smell was terrible. "Dad, it's me, Becky! Get up now, please, Dad!"

She drew the curtains on the lounge front window, which was quite large for an old Welsh country cottage, but it was still small by modern standards. She opened it as wide as it would go and locked it on the old-fashioned stays and then went into the back kitchen.

Part of the reason for the smell became obvious immediately. Kiddy, the old black Welsh sheepdog was cowering by the back door looking decidedly sheepish herself.

"Don't worry about it, old girl, you couldn't help it. He should have let you out hours ago". She opened the back door in and spread the dog's mess further across the lino floor. "Shit!" she said involuntarily as a new, even stronger wave of stench arose from the freshly disturbed and aerated pile of crap.

As soon as the gap was wide enough, Kiddy gratefully slipped out into the garden, happy to be away from the source of her embarrassment.

Becky took a bucket and stinking floor cloth from under the sink, but had to empty the dishes onto the worktop before she could fill the bucket in the sink to clean the floor. In the absence of hot water and proprietary cleaning products, she used cold water and soap powder

There were no rubber gloves either, so she coupied down and began to clean up after the dog.

"Shit, shit, shit and more shit!" she muttered to herself. "This house is one big shithole!" As she moved around the two-foot long brown streak, the soles of her daps stuck to the floor. The whole kitchen needed power-washing with boiling water, she thought.

When she was satisfied with that small patch, Becky went into the garden and the outside toilet and poured the water away. Then she washed her hands and the bucket out under the outside tap; poured bleach from the toilet into it and refilled it with water, leaving the floor cloth to soak and hopefully clean itself.

She re-entered the kitchen, put the plug in the sink, turned on the only tap, opened the window and put the dishes in the water to soak as well. The only cooking utensil that had been used since she had last been there was the frying pan, but all the dishes were dirty and so were a lot of cups, whisky and beer glasses.

She knew what that meant. A fry-up and tea in the morning, late morning or early afternoon; a fry-up and beer in the evening and a few whiskies before bed. The situation was becoming impossible and Becky was rapidly losing patience with her father, although she did feel sorry for his poor old dog for having to live in a pigsty like this with her father, who didn't seem to mind the smell and degradation.

As she was washing the dishes, she looked out on to the short mountain range which rose a few miles beyond what was now euphemistically called a garden, but which had been beautiful when she had lived at home. The mountains had always held a pulling fascination for her; she took after her mother in that regard. Her mother had done the dishes two or three times a day at that window and stared at those mountains for forty-two years.

She and her father liked to think that she was happy playing in or wandering around them now that she was no longer with them. She had died of cancer of the cervix five years before. It had been a complete surprise, because she had never attended the check-ups organised in the hospital. Diagnosed and dead within three months; it had been a terrible shock.

However, these days, Becky knew more about the disease, and had had tests herself, and suspected that her hard-working, stoical mother had known that she had a problem, but she hadn't wanted to be a burden and perhaps quite liked the idea of being dead and away from the drudgery of a small, isolated, lonely, mountain farm.

"I was going to do them as soon as I came down!"

"Oh! You gave me a shock! I do wish you wouldn't creep up behind me like that. I've told you about it before, haven't I, Dad?"

"That's a nice way to greet your old Da, I'm sure. Anyway, I wasn't creeping about and even if I were, I am allowed to in my own house".

"How are you feeling today, Da?" She sometimes lapsed into the old vernacular and called him 'Da' and sometimes they even spoke Welsh, but not so often since Becky had come back from horticultural college and her mother had died.

"I'm all right. I just get so tired and I can't see the point of getting up early when it's cold. Why not wait for the sun to warm the place up a bit first and stay in bed? Is there any tea? I'm parched. My mouth tastes like a labourer's jockstrap".

"Do you have to be so disgustingly graphic? I haven't got two pairs of hands, you know! I had to clean up after poor old Kiddy because you were too 'tired' to let her out, and this place was too filthy to eat anything out of.

"And you really ought to take more care of yourself", she said turning and looking him up and down. "You look a complete mess".

William Jones was standing before her in his pyjama bottoms without any slippers. His half a head of white hair was sticking up at all angles and the muscles in his face looked as if they were still asleep. A whiff of his breath as he spoke revealed that she had been right about the whisky nightcaps – probably enough for a full headdress.

"Why don't you brush your teeth and swill some water over your face to wake yourself up?"

"I don't need any lectures on personal hygiene from you, thank you very much. I have my own routines, established over sixty years and they have always been good enough. I won't be changing them now, not for you nor anyone else. Your dear old mother never complained and her standards are good enough for me.

"Anyway, if you must know the ins and outs of a cat's arse, I was just on my way to use the lavvy. So, if you'll excuse me…"

He went outside. He had always washed under the outside tap unless there was snow or ice on the ground, and a shower or a bath were still once-a-week, special occasions.

She dried her hands on a tea towel, filled the kettle, lit the gas under it, dropped three teabags into the teapot, after checking that it was empty, and went back to the dishes.

"Go and put some clothes on, Da", she prompted him when he came back in and reached for the towel hanging on a hook behind the back door. "I'll make us some toast and the tea will be brewed by then. Go on now, and don't take too long about it".

She warmed the pot, put the teabags in and poured the water onto them, then she pulled the plug from the sink and lit the grill. She had brought her own food as she usually did, because William rarely made it to the shops, and the inside of his fridge was an offence against decency. She would have to tackle it later, but she wanted to have had her breakfast first.

As the grill was warming up, she remembered the dog, and put the scraps she had brought into her bowl. There would probably be a half-opened, half-used, dried-up tin of dog food in the fridge, but that would have to wait and Kiddy deserved a treat from time to time.

Just before she heard her father starting to come downstairs, she shook the tablecloth outside the front door, replaced it with a new one and laid the breakfast out.

"See, you can look nice when you want to, Da".

"No-one's going to see me, so what does it matter? You didn't put any beer with that melted cheese".

"No, you get through enough beer during the day without having to have it for breakfast as well".

"Beer in cheese is not like drinking beer, it's traditional. Welsh Rarebit, that is. It's a centuries-old Welsh custom, but you likes your melted cheese the English way, without beer".

"One day, you will just be grateful, and the shock will be so much that I'll keel over and go to join Mum on the mountains out the back. Parents complain that children are ungrateful, but old people, or you anyway, are much worse".

"I'm sorry, Becky" he said looking up at her. "I do appreciate everything you do for me, really I do… It's just that old people become set in their ways. My mother, may God rest her Soul, always put beer in the melted cheese for my old Dad, and your mother always did it for me. After sixty years of cheese and beer on toast, you becomes set in your ways. You can see that, can't you?"

"Yes, Da, now will you please shut up about the bloody beer!"

"Ooh! Language, Becky! Your mother would not abide foul language in the house and nether will I in her honour! That's another nasty habit you picked up in that English college".

"No, it isn't! I get that from you".

William wasn't sure whether that was true or not, but decided not to argue. "It's a lovely drop of tea, and the cheese is a nice change, if we only 'as it like this once in a while", he said.

"The truth is, I knew there was probably beer in the fridge, but I couldn't bring myself to go in there until after I had eaten".

Her father laughed. "Now that I can understand! I don't like going in there myself… especially if it's dark. You don't know what might be lurking in there. Something might bite your hand off!" and he made a grab for one of her hands.

She pulled it back in time joining in the fun.

"Why do you live like this, Da? There's no need for it, is there? You talk about tradition, but Mum used to keep this house spotless. It was her pride and joy, but I bet she'd be too ashamed to set foot in it now".

"Well, that's where you are wrong, Miss Smarty-Pants with your English college education. I often sit and talk to your mother within these walls".

"I know, Dad, but I bet she's often shaking her head at the state you allow the place to get into. It stank like a cesspit this morning… beer, whisky, dog's mess and old rotting food. It nearly made me sick!"

"I'm sorry, I do know that I let the place go too far sometimes. There is just no incentive any longer though. I try sometimes, I really do. The will power is just not there anymore, I suppose".

"Why don't you come and stay with us? We would love to have you and we have asked you many times. This place is too big for one man alone, especially one like you who has never had to run a household for himself. You're not up to it, Dad, what with your rheumatism, your bad back, and swollen feet".

"You make me sound fit for the knackers yard. Look, I know you have, you have all been very kind, but I cannot leave this house. There are too many people and memories here for me and old Kiddy. Anyways, if we moved out, your mother would be here all alone".

"I know you believe that, Dad, but I think that if there are ghosts, and I don't see why there shouldn't be, then they can go where they like. They won't be tied to one location".

"Well, I am not so sure. You often hear of a spot or house being haunted, don't you? Now I'm not one for emotive language like haunting and such like, but I think that ghosts, like people, become attached to one place and stay there".

"But why would they become attached? It doesn't make any sense".

"Yes, it does when you thinks about it. We with a body become attached to friends, family and our property. If I died tomorrow, it doesn't mean that you would go and live in Zimbabwe, does it? If a meteor came crashing down on this old farm, I wouldn't up sticks and move to Scotland, would I?

"No, of course not. I am emotionally attached to this place. I stay here and if I have to go away for a while, I come back. So do ninety percent of other people. It's only the weird expats who move away for a long time and most of them die at home too. You take it from me that ghosts, or people without bodies, do things for the same reasons as those with bodies".

"Have you actually seen Mum and spoken to her face to face?"

"That's a very difficult question to answer, my dear. I was talking to you this morning, but you had your back to me and couldn't see me. However, that didn't prevent you from knowing that it was me behind you, did it? In answer to your question though, I have never seen her as I am looking at you now, or had a conversation like this. I think that I have caught glimpses of her though, like when the telly's on the blink and I hear her voice in my head".

"You see Mum on the TV? I've seen that in films, but I've never heard of it happening in real life. Are you sure?"

"No, I didn't mean that at all! I might see an image of her in a window, the steam of the kettle or in the shadows of the house. I have a theory about that. Your mother hasn't learned how to project herself yet, and I don't know what I'm looking for. Do you understand?"

"I'm not sure. When you're dead you're dead, aren't you?"

"People assume so, but none of us really knows, do we? Or I'll rephrase that... nobody can prove that they know. There is a man who insists that he is God's right hand man on the planet, but God hasn't helped him prove it. Yet, it is blasted out to the world from Catholic media as if it is undisputed gospel. How can he or they get away with that in this day and age?"

"If there is reincarnation, we have been dead before, so what is there to learn?"

"By the same token, if there is reincarnation, we have been born before, but we still have to relearn how to walk and talk and behave. Perhaps, dead people have to relearn how to make their bodies brighter or denser so that we can see them. Same with their voices".

"So why don't lots of people see lots of ghosts all the time?"

"I think that they do, but we don't hear about it. The Christian Church is very strong and supports the state in most cases, so the state supports it. They prop each other up and the establishment figures who own the press and the media have a large stake in society as it is, so they all stick up for one another. I'm sure that there are tens of millions of Indians who see and talk to ghosts every day. I bet there are millions doing it every day in every country, but they would rather tell you about some jihad or that the pope kissed some tarmac. It's a conspiracy and one that has been going on for centuries or more like when they started persecuting witches".

"Do you really think so, Dad? It sounds a bit far fetched, doesn't it?"

"That is exactly what they want you to think! If they can destroy your argument by ridiculing you, not necessarily your argument itself, then they have an easy victory. I do now, yes, but I've only just come to this conclusion. I have a lot of time to think these days, now that your mother isn't trying to get me to paint the door or repair the roof every time it looks as if I might be taking ten minutes rest".

"Mum wasn't like that!"

"She bloody well was, you know, but she's not now. She had a very hard life, and neither of us helped her as much as we could have, so she made me work hard too. Look, I'm not saying that she was wrong to do what she did. It made all our lives better, but she did do it and sometimes, I went to the pub rather than sit here and get nagged just because I was taking a few hours off. She could not bear to see someone not working. That was old school... it was normal back then. I'm not complaining. I had a few afternoons in the pub, and that was enough, and a darn sight more than she ever had".

"Talking about work, I'd better crack on. I'll wash the lino in the kitchen and clean out the fridge, but I'll have to go home then and start on my own house. Why don't you bring a chair to the kitchen door so we can have a chat?"

"Aye, all right. I can't get down on the floor to clean it any more, or I wouldn't get back up".

"You've never cleaned a floor in your life, but if you wanted to, you would buy a mop or a Squeegee. In fact, I'm going to get you one for Christmas for saying that!"

"You know me too well, that's your trouble. Anyways, we had a strict division of labour, your mother and me. I worked the farm and she ran the house".

"Yes, except that she had to run the vegetable and the herb gardens too".

"Naturally, that was always a part of the house. It was where the wise old women', the witches I was talking about earlier, used to grow their herbs to keep the family strong and healthy. That was not male chauvinism, they wanted and needed that herb patch. So, learn your facts before you go criticising what you don't know nothing about".

"OK, OK, I give up. There, that's the floor done, and it would take half the time with a decent mop. Now for the fridge". She looked at her father, crossed herself and opened the door.

"I'm going in", she said. "Jeez, it's Hell in here!"

"Don't exaggerate", he laughed. "Pass me a beer, leave the rest there and throw everything else out, if you like", which was what she did.

"OK, I really do have to go now. I'll be back tomorrow morning to change the bed and do the lounge. What are you doing this afternoon, can I drop you anywhere?"

"I'll have to think about that... Now then, what have I got on my social calendar for this fine summer's day. Oh, dear, I seem to have mislaid it. What on Earth am I going to do now? I can't remember a single appointment. In that case, I'll just have to rely on the old standby, and walk Kiddy around the hilltop until we are both hungry enough to eat again and come home again to tell Mam all about our walk - how many rabbits we saw, how many snakes, and how many people, which is usually none.

"It's either that or get you to drop us at the village pub and hope that someone will drop us home. Decisions, decisions! It's all go, isn't it?"

"I don't know, but I have to go, and that is certain. Do you want me to pick up your pension tomorrow, Dad, and food and beer?"

"Yes, please, darling. We'll just go for a walk today. Perhaps we'll go to the pub tomorrow. Thanks for all you've done. Let me walk you to your car. Give my love to all your family, won't you? Now, where's that dog of mine?"

"Kiddy! Kiddy! Dewch yma - Come here." she heard him calling as she drove slowly away, watching him and his faithful dog in the rear-view mirror. She wondered how much longer he would be able to cope on his own miles from anywhere as he was.

When Becky had driven off, William went back into the house, locked the back door and took his stick from the corner where it rested and a lightweight jacket from the hook on the front door.

"Bye-bye, my lovely Sarah. I won't be long", he whispered, and locked that behind him too

He didn't need a lead for his dog because she had been a working sheep dog all her life and was always at William's beck and call. They loved each other as much as any two different species can and set off on one of their daily routes which would have taken them near most of their sheep five years before, but now only led to empty grassland. He checked the sky again out of habit, but concluded that it would be a lovely day for the third time that morning.

2. WILLY'S WALK

William bent over despite a twinge of back pain to inspect the soil. There had been a little rain the day before and he didn't want to have to cope with wet grass or slippery mud. It was still soft to the touch, so he chose to walk along the road that day and head upwards towards the summit of the hill that they lived on. His was not the only farm on this hill, but there was none higher than his, so from here on up, he considered it to be 'Jones Peak', although only by default, not by law.

His family had lived in that farm for at least eight generations according to the family Bible, the earliest date in which was 1742. All Joneses and all shepherds. The only change that had taken place in thousands of years was the road, which the government had paid for during the early years of the Second World War so that they could drive a spotter team to the summit to look out for sneaky incoming German planes.

It had been a complete waste of time and money and seemed symbolic of the whole war itself. The only people who had benefitted from the road were his own family, although at the time, his grandfather and grandmother had not wanted it there in case it encouraged tourists and other unwelcome outsiders. They need not have worried. William rarely encountered more than one or two cars a month and they were always owned by villagers wanting to take their dogs for a walk or their family for a picnic.

He and his wife, Sarah, had done that with their Becky when she was still in school too. They had tried to find the time for an outing, for that was their euphemism for it, at least once a month. He had never owned a car though, so a lot depended on the weather which was as unpredictable as the sea.

The mountains formed an efficient windbreak against the worst of the Atlantic weather, but the wind, mist and drizzle that got over them landed on Jones' Peak, from where they would descend down the hill to envelope the village, which he would be able to see in thirty minutes as they rounded that side on their corkscrew journey upwards.

He checked his bearing and stood up straight. He had been finding recently that he had a tendency to stoop if he didn't keep take care. He didn't want that. He used a staff, but he always had done, ever since he was a boy. You could not be a proper shepherd or even an amateur hill walker without a decent staff. In the old days, he had used it to frighten off the occasional snake and tap a dawdling sheep, but he had never used it to help him walk, not like he did these days.

He watched Kiddy race on ahead on the other side of the road – the safer side, away from the edge. She didn't care for the view down like he did and preferred the soft grass beneath her pads. She had caught the smell of something and was looking for its source behind the rocks and boulders that lay scattered about. She was twelve years old, and so was technically older than he was by nearly twenty years, but she could still manage a turn of speed. A short burst when the excitement of the chase took her. This would probably be a rabbit or a hare, but she would chase off snakes too.

It was a darn sight more than he could do these days, he thought sadly. He couldn't even chase a pretty girl nowadays, but worse still, he wouldn't even want to.. Where had all his energy gone? He had been able to run up and down this hill as much as he had wanted to for decades and now he was having trouble walking up the last section with a straight back and a stick.

It was at times like these, when he was alone, which was most of the time now, that he wondered what the point of it all was.

In a hundred yards, he would come to the boulder where he had first kissed Sarah, and where two years later she had accepted his proposal of marriage and made him the happiest man alive. He had never told anyone about that rock, because he was sure that his father would have told him that it had not always been there; that the army bulldozer had pushed all the rocks to the inside of the road rather than carry them down.

He would have said something to spoil the memory and the dream that that smooth rock had been there for ever, or at least since the Ice Age, which was long enough ago for him to still think of as romantic. He had never witnessed one tender moment between his grandparents, on either side, or his own parents. They had been tough, hard, no-nonsense people, suited to their times, whereas he had had the relative luxury of growing up in the post-war years when there was hope and prosperity. Not that it had affected or even reached their little hill, but it was evident in the media that a New World had dawned.

"About bloody time!" he remembered his father saying one day. "I hope it's a bloody sight better than the old one!" His mother had scolded him for bad language and he had taken his pipe out into the back garden 'for a bit of peace'.

He reached the boulder gratefully and sat down. Kiddy put her paws to the surface beside him, stared at him with her still-bright eyes, surrounded by white-grey hair and panted. William was almost panting too, but he stroked her hair, as he had Sarah's all those years ago, and she was just as happy as his then future wife had been.

"There's a good girl. You're a good girl you are. A good girl!" and Kiddy appeared to show satisfaction with the praise by licking his forearm. He gazed out across the narrow road and wide valley before him. "My Mam and Da used to tell me that witches, fairies and pixies live in these hills and valleys… and my grandparents did! And I believed them…" he said to his dog. "Until I became all grown up and educated.

"I didn't want to seem like a stupid farm boy then… I was a New Man in a New World and the Old World was for silly old people. Aye, and so were the witches and The Fair Family – Y Tylwyth Teg. But, it's funny, you know, Kiddy, my girl, the older I got the more them old stories made sense to me… and now? I fair believes 'em again.

"Are you with the Fair People, my lovely Sarah or are you back in the cottage. I would like to think that you're sitting by me on our love seat of stone now…"

Tears did not come, but he thought that they would have in 'normal' people. 'Too much of my Da in me to cry in public!' he said aloud, but only because there was no other human being for miles around.

"I'm a silly old bugger, that's what I am, aren't I, Kiddy? A stupid, silly old bugger… Come on, let's get on with it".

He slid off the rock to his feet and the dog put her front paws on his thigh, looking for another pat and thrashing her tail because she could feel her master's mood lightening. They set off and he checked his posture again.

Thirty-odd minutes later, they were walking across the patch of concrete on the summit of Jones' Peak, or Bryn Teg – Fair Hill – to give it its real name. His goal was the bench in the corner of the concrete slab. In his earliest memories of the hilltop, the small shed where the army lookouts could get out of bad weather had still been there and when it had fallen into disuse, courting couples had taken it over.

After years of complaints from parents, and more than a few shotgun weddings, the council had taken it down. It still made him smile to remember a letter some wag had sent in to the readers' opinion column. He had likened the shed to a pimple on the bald spot of a middle-aged man's head. Well, the pimple had disappeared now and to mark its historical role was this park bench. If you sat on it with your back to the mountains, you felt as if you were sitting on top of the world and could see for miles.

As for the courting couples, they still went there but they all had cars these days, and contraception, or most of them anyway.

It was a lovely day. There was the inevitable breeze, but it was as weak as it got. It made his hair fly about, but it was exhilarating and made him feel glad to be alive again, although he knew that the effect was only temporary. As soon as they left that magical spot, he would wonder what it was all about again. He had known when he had had a family, but he couldn't remember any longer.

"Come on, my lovely girl, let's be heading back down". It was a signal to her for a treat before starting for home. William usually took an apple or a bar of chocolate with him for energy for the homeward journey and he always gave his dog a biscuit as well. She came over to him wagging her tail in expectation.

"Good girl, Kiddy", he soothed stroking her head with one hand while she ate the biscuits out of the other. "That's the lot, off we go".

As William was getting up, a car appeared on the concrete and it flashed its lights. A man of William's age got out and so did a young girl.

"Hello, Bill. The number of times I come up yer and don't see anyone. Anyway, I'm glad I've bumped into you actually. It's my birthday today and I'm having a little do in the village pub. I'm just showing my granddaughter the magnificent view from our hill, then I'll take her home and go on down. Do you fancy it?"

"I don't know, Dai. Happy Birthday by the way". He waved at the girl who remained the other side of the car stroking the dog.

"Come on, I'll take you and your dog down in the car. Better than watching daytime TV, surely?"

"It is that without a doubt. Yes, go on then. My daughter asked me if I wanted to go down this morning. I said 'No, I'll leave it till tomorrow', but this is a good reason to change my mind. You're on!"

"Good man! Good man! If you'd been on the phone I would have rung you to give you an invite, but you won't have one will you?"

"No fear! Bloody waste of money up yer, man… nothing works. No signal, no bloody electric half the time neither".

"No, the world that time forgot, that's where you live. It's like going back a hundred years up yer… maybe two hundred…"

"If it wasn't for this concrete slab, nothing has changed for thousands of years, Dai, thousands and thousands".

When Dai had shown his granddaughter around the hilltop, he promised her an ice cream and they all got into the car to start their descent.

That old dog of yours pongs a bit, doesn't she, Bill? Don't you think it's time she had a bath?"

"No, I do not! She is a farm working girl, not some floozy. She wants to smell like a dog so other dogs will find her attractive, not like some city girl. You won't find another dog readier to jump into a stream than old Kiddy, but I ain't putting no powders and perfumes on her so's people thinks she smells nice. I don't believe in poncifying dogs.

"She's a dog, and if you wants a dog, you 'as to accept that dogs don't smell like us".

Dai looked at his friend and agreed, but wondered whether his friend didn't need a little 'poncifying' himself.

Dai drove past a shop near the village, bought his granddaughter an ice cream and took her home, then they walked a little further on down the hill to the 'Bryn Teg', the village public house. It was nearly four o' clock.

William entered the pub first, but turned to hold the door open for his friend without looking inside. As Dai walked through the door, the sound of 'Happy Birthday' erupted. They both looked around the bar in amazement at the decorations and trimmings. The landlord and landlady, Harry and Joyce, led the birthday song accompanied by ten or twelve men and women, all of about retirement age.

"Well I never!" he said to everyone as he and William took stools at the bar and Kiddy lay down in her usual spot under a table by the door.

"Pint of bitter, Dai?" asked Harry.

"Yes, please, Harry. Who did all this?"

"It was Joyce's idea, but a few of your friends here helped us decorate the place. Bitter for you too, Bill?"

"Aye, thanks, Harry. I'll get these".

"Happy Birthday, mate!" he said clinking glasses with his friend when their pints had arrived, "and many more of them".

"Thanks, Bill. All the best, mate. I'm glad you could come. I wasn't expecting all this though and that's for sure. Thanks for all the trouble you've gone to for my birthday, everyone", he said standing up and raising his glass to everyone. "I don't think I've had a birthday party since the kids left home. It was a very kind thought. Thank you, Joyce".

When the initial excitement caused by Dai's entrance had died down, most of the men went back to watching a rerun of a recent football game, while others exchanged anecdotes about village life and hill farming in general.

"Fancy a game of Crib, Dai?"

"Sure. Usual stakes?"

"Aye, penny a point. Harry, the cards, please".

Harry nodded and reached for the set. He knew what they were talking about because they had been playing Crib together for all of the nineteen years he had been the landlord of the Bryn Teg, and he had been told that they had been playing it for just as long before he had taken over.

"Shall I give Kiddy her usual as well?" asked Harry.

William looked over his shoulder to see his dog panting back at him, her tail wagging as usual whenever he paid her attention.

"Yes, please, Harry. It's her wages for having to wait for me, and she's come to expect them now".

"How long has she been coming here? Ten years?"

"Twelve, but she wasn't what you would call a regular until I sold the flock five years ago".

"Twelve years, is it? Doesn't time fly?" he said pouring a half a bitter into the bowl that William left behind the bar for her, and topping it up with water. He put that and a packet of Smokey-Bacon flavoured crisps on the bar and walked around the counter.

"There you are, old girl", he said putting the bowl on yesterday's newspaper and emptying the crisps onto it. Kiddy waited patiently, her tail wagging and her tongue hanging out. The moment that Harry had finished patting her head, she tucked into her treat.

"I love to do that for her. I actually look forward to it", said the kind-hearted landlord.

The afternoon passed quickly, and after several games, most of which Dai won for a change, William made ready to go.

"Not going already are you, Bill?"

"Aye, I've had my three pints and two hours and you've had my money - birthday boy's luck, so it's time to hit the road".

"Aw, come on, I'm enjoying winning for a change. I'll tell you what, stay another hour and not only will I buy you a pint, but I'll give you double stakes".

"Oh, I don't know", he said but he was considering the proposition. His friend had not had to buy a drink all afternoon and he had ninety-eight pence of William's money.

"All right, but I got to take the dog outside for a Gypsy's first. Her bladder's not as strong as it used to be".

"You could say that about all of us", replied Dai. "You do that and I'll nip to the gents' as well".

Kiddy coupied down in the car park and looked away from William shyly as she always did when going about her business and then started to walk home. William whistled and held the door open for her. She hurried inside and they both resumed their places.

"I needed that", said Dai holding the deck of cards out for William to cut them, "and it looked as if she did too".

"She thought she was going home for her dinner, so I'll only stay another hour. Cheers, Dai. Thanks for the pint".

"My pleasure", he replied.

"I'll get my money back out of you now".

"Never! I'm going to whip your arse. I'm on a roll, I can feel it".

Ninety minutes and two pints later, William got up to go again, and Dai didn't try to stop him.

"A quick visit to the bog, and then we're off. I won't get home until eight o'clock now. I'm not as fleet of foot as I used to be you know. Oh, and a packet of peanuts, Harry, please".

"None of us are, mate. Thanks for the lesson in Crib, but I nearly had you this time. You're a jammy sod, you get some incredible luck, you do!"

"That's skill, my boy! I've been trying to teach you the game for forty years. Don't you think it's time you packed it in and tried snooker instead?"

"I'll have you next time".

"In your dreams. Enjoy the rest of your birthday. Bye everyone, time to get up that hill and home". He looked around the room, but already knew that no-one could give him a lift even part the way home. When he opened the door, Kiddy was in front of him.

Kiddy usually led the way out of the village, and he would follow on two and a half yards behind her. He had never been sure why she liked to walk like that, but he suspected that she was trying to force the pace. When they got onto the hill road, she wandered more freely ahead, behind and to the right of him.

Five pints was more than William was accustomed to these days and it made him sing to himself quietly as he tried not to trudge up the hill. He liked to sing the hymns that he had learned in school and chapel. He didn't know a single modern song, except for some Max Boyce that they sang in the pub during a rugby international, and he was proud of it. Most of the hymns he could sing in Welsh and English, but preferred the Welsh versions.

Forty minutes later, William was approaching a corner which would reveal another rock that they always rested at on the downhill side of his house. He felt his jacket pocket for the packet of peanuts he would share with Kiddy before they tackled the last short leg home. It was more of a treat to stop there than a necessity. They both enjoyed their breaks, their snacks and taking their time in their new lives of retirement. As he rounded the corner, he was wondering where Kiddy had got to. It wasn't like her not to check up on him every few minutes.

Then he saw her. She was lying on the ground just before the rock. It immediately struck him as strange that she wasn't sitting in her usual place on the right-hand side of it.

He hurried his pace. Fifty yards from her, she gave a kick, arched her back and was still. He started to run and called her name, but she made no attempt to respond.

He dropped to his knees hurting them on the hard surface, but the tears were not because of that. He could see that his friend had suffered a heart attack and not survived it.

William drew her up onto his lap and wept like a child. Some thirty or forty minutes later, he scooped her up with his right hand and tried to stand up, but he could not. His knees were too weak, so he crawled to their rock and used his left hand to help him up. He sat on the rock with his dog on his lap and the tears started again. 'She hadn't even had her peanuts!' he was thinking as a pain grew in his left arm. The iron grip of a vice squeezed his chest and he was groaning as he and Kiddy slipped off the rock onto the sparse grass below it.

3. SARAH

"Where am I?" asked William of the people standing around him. "Am I in hospital?"

"Yes, you can call it that. You are very sick, but you have recovered a great deal since we found you, so there is every reason to believe that you will make a total recovery".

"Thank you, doctor. My mind is a little foggy. I think I must have a hangover. I had a little more than usual to drink... It was a friend's birthday..."

"Yes, we know, but don't worry about anything like that now you need rest more than anything".

"Kiddy, my dog, died, didn't she?"

"Don't worry about her either. She is in good hands. We are taking good care of her too. You will be able to see her again shortly".

"I don't understand… who found me? Nobody goes up on the hill at that time of night. I must have been very lucky... Oh, unless it was a courting couple..."

"Please", said the doctor "try to rest. You will learn everything you want to know in good time, but not now".

"All right, doctor, you know best. I am very tired. So long as my Kiddy is all right I'm happy... I don't know what I would do without her..."

William drifted off into a deep sleep in which he felt warm and comfortable. Kiddy was at his feet with her head on his knee.

When he awoke he felt a lot better.

"I had a great sleep", he said to the woman at his bedside. "I'll know better than to drink that much again... my head has cleared though. Did I have a heart attack? Is that what landed me in here?"

The woman drew closer allowing him to see her clearly for the first time. "Hello, Willy. Yes, you would call it a heart attack".

He scrutinised her face and figure. "You look very much like my wife did at your age. She was the only person who ever called me Willy. It was her pet name for me, her private joke. She never once used it in public, because of its, er, connotations, if you know what I mean. In those days, women were a lot more modest in public".

"Yes, the good old, bad old days, eh, Willy?"

"It's amazing, the likeness, I mean, it's amazing. You could be my wife's daughter or younger sister. Do you have any relatives in Bryn Teg?"

"We are a big family, I have relatives almost everywhere". Her smile broadened as if she had told a cryptic joke.

"What is it? Come on, you can tell me. Have I got food stuck in my teeth? You know, the more we talk, the more I feel that we have met before".

"Do you really not recognize me, Willy? I can assure you that we have done a lot more than just meet. That would be some euphemism!" This time she laughed out loud.

"Sarah? But how can it be you? I mean if you're Sarah, doesn't that mean that I am dead as well?"

"Does it, Willy? You tell me. You were telling Becky only this morning that we have spoken many times in the cottage".

"Yes, all right, but this is different... I can see and talk to you now as if you were really here..."

"I am really here. I never really left. Oh, I could have gone away... many people do, perhaps even most, but I couldn't leave you all on your own. Did you think that I would?"

"No, I just thought that we probably had to learn how to communicate again..."

"Yes, there is a lot of truth in that, but people have to want to do it as well, which is why most people only see friends and relatives".

"So, er, can we really be together?"

"We are together..."

"Yes, but I mean really together..., er, like man and wife... like we used to?"

"No, I am afraid not, not yet, Willy. For the time being, there is a barrier between us that neither of us can cross, but one day that barrier will come down. I promise you that".

"You mean when I'm dead?"

"If you want to put it like that, yes, but we don't like to use that word. It is so full of negative content, don't you think? 'Dead' - there, I've said it, but it's like the 'N-word' or the 'C-word' is for others. It's unpleasant, unnecessary and there are better ways of expressing the concept. Do you see what I mean? Do I look dead to you? Is the flesh falling from my bones? Are my eyes hanging out of their sockets? Do I look like a zombie from the Walking Dead?"

"No, you look as beautiful as ever you did".

"Thank you, and why would I choose to look any other way to my darling husband?"

"I can't imagine".

"No, nor can I. So, why do people think that that's what ghosts do? Really, it is quite beyond me - all of us, in fact".

"Yes, well, when you put it like that... I shalln't use that word again".

"Good, thank you, my dear".

"So, Sarah, if we can't do, er, anything together, what can we do? Oh, where are we first?"

"We are in a place that people in this part of the world used to call Annwn. You have heard that name before, haven't you?"

"Hell, isn't it? Jesus, I didn't think that you or I would be going there!"

"No, it is not Hell. When the early Christians heard that we Celts believed that Annwn was under the ground, they tried to convince us that it was the same as their Hell, but it is not true. In fact, Hell doesn't exist either. As for an exact location, we are under and within the mountains and hills that surround our lovely cottage. However, in a way that is only an illusion too. We could be anywhere we wanted to be. Is that any clearer?"

"As clear as ditch water, my love".

"I am afraid that it takes some people longer than others to grasp the concept. It is extraordinary how long it takes some, you know. Do you remember the one they called King Henry VIII when he was last on Earth? Well, he's been here for about four hundred and fifty years, I think - history was never my strong point, as you know. Anyway, he has a Welsh connection so we took him in long before I got here, yet he is still wandering around shouting at people, and ordering them about. 'I'm the King of England,' he screams, 'and I will be obeyed!' I shouldn't laugh really, but it is so funny. Most people either ignore him or avoid him, but sometimes someone will bow or curtsey to him just for a laugh. We've got a few nutters like him.

"Most people get the gist of things after a while though. Would you like me to show you around later?"

"Yes, Sarah. I would like that. Will I be able to get up and walk around so soon after a heart attack?"

"You did ought to have more rest first, but nobody here would do anything to further endanger your health. Trust me on that".

"Oh, I trust you, Sarah, I always have. You are the best friend I have ever had, which reminds me. The doctor said that I could see Kiddy later. Is that now?"

"Yes, if you want. You are well enough for her. One second, please".

Sarah stood up and opened a door that he had not noticed up until that moment. Kiddy bounded in wagging her tail.

"Hello, girl, how are you?" She jumped up onto the bed and lay alongside his body.. William wanted to stroke her head, but could not seem to make his hands do it.

"She has been such a comfort to me, since you, er, passed over".

"I know, but you were never truly alone for long and after my return to here, there has always been someone with you".

"I was sure that you were there, but I didn't feel anyone else".

"Oh, there were many... your parents, your grandparents on both sides, that girl who fancied you in school - I forget her name now...".

"Gwladys..."

"That's the one... and many, many more besides".

"I didn't notice them, I only had eyes for you, my love".

"You always were a smooth talker, but thanks for saying it. It still feels nice. We are supposed to try to lose those Earthly pleasures, but everyone agrees that it takes ages…. which reminds me. How on Earth could you allow our lovely home to look and smell like it does? Becky is an absolute saint for taking care of you the way she does. Don't you realise that she has her own family to take care of? I try not to feel shame and embarrassment any more, but you have managed to make me feel them. I didn't know what to say when I saw other people like me going to check up on you. Really, William, you must make more of an effort to take good care of yourself! And poor old Kiddy had to live in that mess as well. You should be ashamed of yourself, William, for subjecting your friend to those conditions".

"I'm sorry, old girl", he said trying again to stroke her head. "The dog, I mean, not you, Sarah. I just never thought about her minding, or that my friends and relatives would see how I was living. I am ashamed to think of it now though".

"And so you should be, but don't dwell on it too much, just live and learn. That's the name of the game".

"Does that mean that my parents are here?"

"Yes, somewhere, but I'm not sure where. I can find out though, if you want".

"No, it's all right for now, perhaps we can meet them later when we go walkabout".

"Yes, all right, my dear, I'll speak to them later".

"I have just noticed how vital Kiddy looks… she has lost her grey hair. Do I look younger too?"

"It is best if I explain something about looks. Here, in Annwn and places like it, your looks are basically an expression of who you are inside, the real you. Since we don't have the heavy physical bodies that we once had, we can appear to others how we feel, and we can modify that to some extent through will power, although most of us don't bother after a while. It is far easier to change the way you think in order to have a beneficial effect on the way you appear than to constantly have to be thinking about moulding your body to how you would like it to look.

"Having said that, those on the Surface remember us in the form we had when we died, which was why you didn't recognise me for sometime earlier, even though I was calling you by my pet name for you. Do you see what I mean? When I came back to the cottage I had to concentrate on making myself appear old and bent so that you would know who I was and not be afraid.

"Believe me, trying to hold a false image for a sustained period is hard work. It takes a lot of strength and a lot of skill obtained through practice, which is why I said that it is better to change from the inside out. Still, when needs must…"

"Is that why you kept shimmering and disappearing?"

"I wasn't aware that I was doing that, but yes, probably. It really is very difficult. I would concentrate on holding the image, go to say something and forget about my appearance. At least I won't have to do that again with you".

"Sorry, you didn't answer my question… Do I look young and handsome again?"

"You'll do for me, my dear, but the short answer is no. You still have your body, and it is old with all that that entails… You know, sagging skin, weak muscles, curved spine, grey hair, drooping fat…"

"Yes, all right I get the picture, and what a handsome one of me it is that you paint too".

"I'm sorry, but we become used to working on the inner person down here and one of the exercises is telling the truth… and you did ask. I didn't volunteer it to hurt you, did I? Anyway, your physical body has sort of moulded the real you inside it, and so without liberation from it and without training, you look just the same here as you do up there.

"No, that is not quite true. Here you are not actually carrying your physical body around with you, so you will probably feel lighter, more nimble, more active, and that will make you happier. You will probably feel twenty years younger when we go out for a look around later".

"That's something to look forward to anyway… But wait a moment! If I am not dead, er, sorry, if I am still alive, and that's what you said right?" She nodded. "Where is my body?"

"It's in hospital".

"I thought the doctor just told me that I am in hospital".

"Yes, he did, but he only agreed with you to avoid having to have this discussion with you himself. We thought that that would be better coming from me".

"So, are you saying that I am not in hospital, but my body is… somewhere?"

"Yes, but you could call this a hospital too, if you wanted to. You are recuperating after a very nasty shock. It's just that we don't deal with physical bodies here. Your other half is in the Cardiff Heath Hospital".

"So, it's over there, about forty miles away, and I'm down here under the mountains?"

"Yes, it is an over simplification, but it will do".

"Will I ever see it again?"

"Oh, yes. You will be reunited with it when it and you have recovered sufficiently. It shouldn't be long".

"OK, I am not worried about that… in fact I'm not worried about anything surprisingly…"

"Good", smiled Sarah, "that's the way we like it".

"It's just that I have so many questions. How did I get here? And how did my body get over there?"

"Ah, good questions.

"I'll deal with you first and then your body, because they are two different stories. I check up on you from time to time during the day and night, as you know, and I knew that you went to the pub with Dai, so I left you to it. Sometime later, I checked at home and when you still weren't there I started down for the village. I came across you and Kiddy by that old resting rock. So, I sort of 'brought you around' using terms that you would understand and called back here for help. The help brought you back here for me, because I could see that it wasn't your time to leave your body for good.

"However, there was nothing we could do for your body, so I hurried to Becky, who was in bed asleep and spoke to her in her dream. I'm afraid I scared her a bit, because she interpreted what I said as a nightmare. She woke her husband John up and told him that she had had a horrible dream that you had collapsed on the road back from the pub – 'dead drunk', was the expression I think she used.

"Anyway, she wouldn't give John any peace, so he told her that he'd mind the kids while she went to check the cottage. I won't tell you what they said about you not having a mobile phone. Still, she found your body easily enough with me standing over it pointing and jumping up and down. I don't know how she got you onto the back seat, but she did, with a little help from me and a helper, and she put Kiddy in the boot and took you to the doctor, who was also in bed.

"You caused quite a stir, I can tell you and you're still the talk of the village today".

"My fifteen minutes of fame, eh?"

"Something like that, yes.

"Anyway, Becky stayed with your body and went to the hospital with it – in fact, she is still there. The poor girl has hardly stopped praying and crying, and John has buried Kiddy's body in our back garden. There was nothing anyone could do for her; she was already gone, but not to worry, eh? She's happy enough, aren't you girl?" she said leaning forward to stroke the dog. It doesn't take animals long to recover, because they haven't got any preconceived notions preventing them from seeing the Truth"

"Yes, she's a great girl. She has been such a comfort to me since you passed away, er, on, or is it over?"

"Replaced by a dog, eh? How fickle men are! Only joking! I'm glad she was there. As for dying, you describe it in any way that you think best illustrates the reality".

"When are we going out, I can't wait to explore this underground world of yours". He swung his legs out from under the sheet and then looked under the sheet. "I haven't got any clothes on".

"Your clothes are in a locker in the hospital, but if you are referring to yourself here and now, the fact is that you have not only got no clothes on, but you haven't got anything on".

"Yes, I have. I've got this sheet".

"Not from where I am sitting".

"Well, what is this then?" he asked holding a corner of the sheet up.

"That and the bed you probably think you're lying on are figments of your imagination, but not of mine. Therefore, you see them, but I do not".

"Say that again, please, Sarah?"

"When you woke up, you were expecting to be in a hospital, so you saw the people around you as doctors and nurses. Furthermore, patients in hospital lie in beds covered by a sheet, so that is what you saw. However, we know that you are not in a hospital for physical bodies and that you are not in a bed covered with a sheet, so we don't see them. You see what you expect to see".

"So, all those people saw me, er, starkers?"

"I don't know how they saw you. It depends on their level of advancement and what they wanted to see".

"So, you are naked too then?"

"What do you see, Willy?"

"It's strange… When I first noticed you, you were in a white nurse's uniform, but when I realised who you were, you were wearing what you have on now – a long white dress and a garland of white flowers in your hair like a crown. The strange thing is, I didn't notice you change…"

"That's because I didn't, your perception of me did, so it was instantaneous, but only in your head. The fact of the matter is, I can let you dress me as you want, and I can dress myself how I want as well and so we can look different to different people at the same time. You haven't had any practice at this yet, but you will soon get the hang of it when you live here.

"I like the long white dress and the garland though, I think I'll keep that for now. As for yourself, Willy, just imagine yourself wearing anything you like and you will be, at least as far as you are concerned. When you become more adept, you will be able to suggest the clothes you are wearing to whoever is looking at you and they will normally accept your suggestion.

"How do you feel, my love? Are you fit enough to go outside?"

"Yes, I feel fantastic. I could eat a horse too. Do you like the clothes?"

"You are funny, Willy!" she said smiling lovingly at him. "I can't see any clothes, I just told you that. I just see my darling Willy".

"Mmm, I'll try not to read too much into that, or I'll never pluck up the courage to go outside. Shall we eat first?"

"Where, in the room or outside?"

"Outside, I think".

"Are you hungry?"

"I'm famished", he said rubbing his stomach.

"Are you sure?"

"No, I'm not", he replied slowly. "Thinking about it, I'm not hungry at all. Leastwise, my body is not hungry, but my brain is saying that it ought to be. I suppose I don't have a body to feel hungry for, do I?"

"Yes, you do, but the doctors in the hospital are feeding it with a drip. However, you are still connected to it, so you can probably feel your stomach shrinking. Let me assure you though, you are not hungry. Not that that stops us eating if we want to. We just get out of the habit. I'll get you something to eat, if you like, though, just say the word".

"OK, let's leave it for now. We'll play it by ear. Lead the way, my dear", he said opening the door for her.

4. ANNWN

When William had closed the door behind him, he turned to see Sarah standing in the middle of a huge expanse of earthen-red nothingness. She was smiling at him quizzically, obviously waiting for something.

"Is this it, Annwn?" he asked.

"Yes, why, what were expecting?" she asked.

"I don't know, I didn't know what to expect..."

"So, you see nothing, eh? Go on, what do you see? Tell me…"

"As you say, nothing, just a reddish darkness".

"A lot of visitors say that. Others say that they see a medieval scene or a kind of Nordic Valhalla..."

"Medieval? Yes... wow!" And there it was before him. They were standing in the courtyard of a subterranean medieval castle with market stalls, horses, cattle, sheep, dogs, adults and children.

"That's amazing! Where did all this come from?"

"It and they were here all the time doing what they are doing now, it is just that you couldn't see them because you were not expecting to see them. Now you know that they are here, they will live their lives before your eyes and you yours before theirs".

"I think I'm getting the hang of this now. Where does the light come from?"

"From your imagination, or look for it and you will see plenty of sources of light. Your imagination will probably see them as torches, windows or even skylights".

"Yes, I see them now, but if they are not the true sources of the light what are?"

"Think about it... Well?"

"The mountains don't exist and our world... Ah, got you! So, there is nothing to block the sunlight... Right!"

"There is nothing to block the sunlight, that is true, but the sun doesn't exist in our world either and we don't need light to see by. People create it with their imaginations because they think that they need it, or ought to have it, or because it comforts them or reminds them of their Earthly existence. It's silly really, but then people are silly, aren't they? Aren't we? I should say, because every single one of us finds ourselves doing or creating something pointless just because it used to be so.

"Like those people shopping for food and those people selling it. Just tell me what they think they need money for in the Afterlife? It's the same with those men drinking in the tavern across the square. They are having a great time talking with their friends, but they haven't realised yet that they don't need to drink beer, or ale, in order to do that anymore. They simply don't have the body parts anymore that alcohol affects... and they would know that, if they bothered to think about it, but they are stuck in a rut, a harmless one though it is".

"They are not hurting anyone, are they, so where's the harm?"

"Oh, no harm to anyone, just no use either. You see, you can't really harm anyone but yourself here. They are wasting their own time".

"Oh, come on! A few hours drinking pointless beer and having a laugh with your mates is not going to play havoc with their Spiritual development, surely!"

"I quite agree. I am not against having fun with friends or even drinking beer with them, but you don't know how long they have been sitting there. It could be five hundred years. Like potty Henry. In five hundred years, you might normally live two, three or even five lives in a body. That is a lot of experience to throw away... Or just think of how much good they could have done. It is not hurting anyone; it is just a sad waste... that's all".

"Yes, when you put it like that, I can seem what you mean. At least on the Surface, we have a few beers, get drunk and go home... five hundred years is a long time..."

"To be honest, I don't know how long that particular group of men has been sitting there, but you hear things, you know... and as for drinking on the Surface, overindulgence is a bad thing wherever it occurs.

"Anyway, enough of that for now. Would you like to look around this place, Willy?"

"What do you call 'this place', Sarah, and how big is it? It doesn't look big enough to hold thousands of years of souls, if that word is acceptable".

"Yes, 'souls' is a good word. I can see that you still haven't quite grasped the concepts yet, but never mind. We all travel at our own speed. Most of us here, let's call it Wales, call this place either Annwn or the Other World, once they have been here a while, although they might have other names for it before they arrive. This actual spot in Annwn is like the capital city of Annwn and it is called Annwn too. As to its size, I shouldn't think that anyone knows exactly how big it is. It is always big enough for the number of people who want to be here.

"However, that number may be a lot fewer than you imagine, because people are being reborn all the time, and some just move on. Another thing is that I might look to you like the wife of five foot five and eight stone that you used to live with, but I don't actually take up any space. I just look as if I do, but that is an illusion, as I told you before.

"Everything and everyone, or their forms at least, are all illusion to make it easier for newcomers... and the drinkers, shoppers and merchants haven't advanced far enough to realise that what they are doing is, well, silly and pointless. Does that make it any clearer?"

"I'm sure I'll get the hang of it. I certainly do envy those men though. I could murder a pint and a Ploughman's Lunch".

"It would be something to tell the boys down the Bryn Teg, wouldn't it, that I had a pint and a Ploughman's Lunch in Heaven with my wife. Come on!"

They crossed the square and entered the bar, the front wall of which opened onto the courtyard. The five men who were sitting at the table, which they had to shuffle past to get to an empty one eyed him suspiciously and her lasciviously. They sat next to each other facing the open wall. The landlord was soon with them.

"Good day, sir, mistress. What will it be?"

"Sarah?"

"Oh, nothing for me thanks. I couldn't eat or drink a thing".

"Oh, yes, right, I see. Um, I'll have a pint of your best bitter, please landlord and a Ploughman's Lunch".

"Bitter?"

"He means ale", said Sarah.

"Ale I got, but what is a Ploughman's Lunch? It's not some fancy Cavalier foreign muck, is it? I don't serve no Cavaliers in 'ere. We's all Roundheads true to a man and I don't want no fighting in 'ere. If you're a Cavalier I'll ask you and your lady to kindly take your custom elsewhere".

"We are not Cavaliers, my good man" said Sarah. "We are loyal Roundheads too, a Ploughman's Lunch, is what our daughter used to call bread, cheese, onion, an apple, and whatever else you happen to have. It's just our family's pet name for it".

"Oh, in that case, I'll see what the missus can rustle up".

The five men at the table were staring at them, but went back to talking in a huddle when the landlord left.

"Roundheads and bloody Cavaliers? That was Oliver Cromwell wasn't it? You were right, nearly five hundred years ago".

"Yes, as I said, word gets around, you know".

A few minutes later, the landlord put an earthenware pint pot of foaming beer and a wooden platter of food in front of them. Is that your ploughman's".

"Yes, it's perfect, thank you".

"I'll have to remember that, a Ploughman's Lunch. That'll be thre'pence then, please, sir".

He looked at Sarah forlornly.

"I didn't think! Money! I haven't got any!"

"Yes, you have. Look in your britches' pocket, I saw three shiny new pennies in there this morning".

He put his hand in his pocket and felt a few familiar coins. He took them out and gave them to the waiting landlord. They were both relieved.

William ate his lunch and drank his beer while his wife looked on smiling, shaking her head from time to time.

"This is gorgeous! It's the best pint and best food I've ever had..., er, since you came here, I mean, my dear".

"Flatterer! Come on let's get out of this time warp, I find it depressing, cloying, and awfully sad, don't you?"

"No, I quite liked it in here. If I'd been on my own I think I would have joined that bunch of lads and asked how the war was going".

"A war that has been over for four hundred and sixty-five years or so? Fascinating? I'm sure. You probably know more about it than they do. What would you like to see now?"

"Is there a chapel? No, silly question, but I have always liked a nice church".

"Why is it a silly question? If we've got pubs, it follows that we would have churches as well".

"All right, lead on, Sarah".

They crossed the courtyard again and stood before a Gothic Church that he had not noticed previously.

"Don't tell me, you hadn't seen it. That is something you will have to get used to. We have many churches and chapels of all denominations here, but this is the one that I think you will like the best".

"You know me well, Sarah. I don't hold with places of worship being over ostentatious. Let's take a look inside".

William held the door open and followed her in. It was a typical Welsh city chapel of the mid-Nineteenth Century. The kind that William would have liked to visit on a rare trip to Cardiff or one of the other cities. He motioned Sarah to sit in a pew at the back and took the place in. There were three people praying at the front, but they didn't pay him any attention, although he was more interested in the stained-glass windows anyway. The larger window was of Jesus on the Cross and the smaller of Mary and Child.

"There's a lovely peaceful atmosphere in here", he said. "Very nice. It never crossed my mind that people would be praying in Heaven though".

"You would be surprised what goes on here", she replied. "A lot of people sitting in churches don't even know that they are dead. I mean that goes for a lot of people in general, but a lot of the old God-fearing types are the worst. Some know that they have passed over, but can't understand why they haven't met St. Peter at a Gate. Others sit on clouds playing harps waiting to be called. It's enough to drive you to despair. They are worse than the Roundheads drinking over there.

"At least they don't know that they have passed on. They were probably killed by an explosion or a cannonball they didn't see coming and haven't worked out what has happened to them yet. Whereas a lot of the faithful old church-goers do know that they have passed on, but can't believe that it is not like their priest told them it would be. And before you guess it, the priests, the monks, the nuns and the popes are the worst.

"We've got thousands of them sitting around shaking their heads wondering why they haven't been called yet. They have a lot to answer for. They lived a distorted life and convinced thousands of millions of others to do the same. It creates a great deal of work for us, you know".

"I'm sorry, Sarah, but you've lost me again. I know that a lot of the clergy are hypocrites, but most of them try to do good..."

"Yes, fair enough, but how can you set yourself up as a teacher if you are not sure of your subject?"

"They have the right to teach what is in the Bible or the Koran or whatever, surely?"

"Yes, but they probably weren't present when those great teachers were telling the Truth, or if they were then they have forgotten. They are teaching from books written by God-knows whom with what agenda? I'm afraid that it's just not good enough to teach from a book that someone tells you is right".

"So those great teachers, as you call them, did exist then?"

"Oh, yes, and Buddha and thousands, perhaps tens of millions more over the eons. The two big distortions in Christianity though are the ideas that Jesus is the only son of God and that he died for everybody's sins. I mean, it's so laughable that it makes even me want to swear. Those two concepts have set more people back on their journey to Understanding than any others, and there are thousands of contestants for the stupidest ideas, believe me".

"I do, Sarah, but why?"

"Well, Jesus was a man who was killed on the Cross. In other words he was just like everyone else in that he died. Then his Spirit got up and walked away from its then useless body, just like everybody else's does. We are all, every single person who has ever been born, a son or a daughter of God. That is why we are all brothers and sisters.

"Secondly, no-one can pay the price of the sins of another person. This is ridiculous. That means that the wickedest person in time only has to say sorry on his deathbed and everything is hunky-dory. No way! That is not how Karma works. Everyone is held accountable for his or her own mistakes and there is no getting out of it, no matter what any book says. That is an immutable law of life.

"Think about it... otherwise it allows people to rob and rape, steal and enchain their way through life, say sorry at the end and go back and do it again next time. No, whoever made that bit up was either wicked or deranged and it wasn't Jesus".

"Have you met Him then? Jesus?"

"No, not yet. He is a very busy man, as are all the great teachers. Everyone wants to meet them, when they realise where they are. I have heard tell that he has been here, but it was before my time".

"Right, I see. I remember you saying now that there are lots of places like Annwn, so he lives somewhere else, does He?"

"Er, yes and no. This is one of those questions. It is easier to comprehend when you give the places different names, but in reality they are all the same place. Like towns in a country, bedrooms in a hotel or rooms in a mansion, as Jesus did say. It is easier to give each location a name or a number, but they are all in the same place or locality. Do you see? I am not sure that I am explaining this well.

"We call this place Annwn and most of us here are Welsh, but Scandinavians call it Valhalla, however, it is the same place and so is Heaven. We think of our place as being underground, so do the Scandinavians, but the majority of Christians think of Heaven as being in the sky. Other peoples think of it being under the sea or on a distant island, but it's all the same place really, but slightly different too.

"Put it this way, the national psyche of the population determines where they think it is and what it looks like... in general, but that can be altered to suit each individual as well. It's like, I might call a colour scarlet, another may say crimson and you may say cochineal, but they are all red".

"So, where is Annwn City then?"

"Mmm, you are making this difficult, aren't you? Never mind though, that is part of my job. Annwn can be wherever you want it to be. Welsh people naturally thought that it would be in Wales. By the way, not everyone thought it to be underground; some thought it to be off the coast.

"Anyway, so, generally speaking, it is in Wales. We come from South Wales, and Bryn Teg in particular, so we want it to be there, and so there it is, but someone from, say, Harlech would want it to be there, perhaps, and so for him or her that is where it would be. Some writers throughout history have told us where it is in their stories, but what they didn't realise was that it is everywhere and anywhere and nowhere, all at the same time".

"So, we are under our mountains?"

"Uh, yes. If we want to be. Yes. Let's just settle for yes, it's a lot easier".

"I like it down here, but it is rather weird, isn't it?"

"In fact, this is normal... what is up there is weird. Measured in Earth years, souls spend more time in the Other World, than 'up there', but I agree. It does take a bit of getting used to again and as you have seen, some people take centuries to do it".

"How long have we got to learn? I mean time is infinite, isn't it"

"Oh, yes! Time is the least of people's worries. You literally have all the time in the world and more. No-one's time will ever run out. That is not the problem. The problem is when people realise how much time they have wasted and what their real purpose is. It comes as a huge shock to a lot of people. One day, everyone realises, so I am assured, and most of them suffer a period of intense remorse - especially society's self-declared 'teachers', the priests. They have a very hard time of it. It is pitiful to watch".

"You have seen this?"

"Yes, many times".

"I am glad that I have had you to put me straight, Sarah".

"Thank you. It is my pleasure to be of help".

"Wait a minute though... I have you to, er,...

"Guide..."

"Yes, to guide me, but what about all the others we have spoken of like the Roundheads?"

"Everyone has a Guide, A Spirit Guide, according to their interest in learning and that changes with time. I am not actually your Spirit Guide, but it is natural for someone to take an interest in someone they care about".

"Thank you, my love. So, who is my Spirit Guide?"

"I am sorry, but it is up to him or her to reveal himself to you and up to you to listen when he calls you. Sometimes, Guides get bored when they have been ignored for a long time and drift off. They are not supposed to, but who can blame them? It is like being put on hold for an hour by the gas board".

"So, is that a sort of job then down here?"

"Yes, but I would rather go into that later, if you don't mind. Let's get out of here. How would you like to visit my school?"

"Yes, sure. I suppose you mean where you go to school, or do you mean teach?"

"No, I mean where I go to school. I would like to teach one day, but for the moment that is still a long way off. In the scheme of things, I've only been here ten minutes".

"To me it has been five long years, Sarah".

"Has it been that long really? With no sun, and infinity to work with, we don't track time in quite the same way as you do. We tend to think in terms of progress not hours".

"It's funny, we don't think of ghosts going to school. Ghost School. It has a certain ring to it doesn't it? Learn how to spook your neighbours and make dogs howl in the night in three terms. Grants available for the needy".

"Very funny, I'm sure! It's nothing like that. What I find funny now is that people on the Surface think that when they die they will become omniscient angels and that some other people might become ghouls or ghosts. Did I use to think like that as well, Willy?"

"I don't remember ever discussing it with you. We didn't have a lot of time for philosophising, did we?"

"No, I guess not. Come on in, it's up those stairs".

5. SEAT OF LEARNING

"Take you sandals off, that's right, and put them in one of these pigeon holes. Now walk through this bath of water and shuffle your feet on the towelled step to dry them".

He copied Sarah. There was a shallow stone foot bath between the door, which was pinned back open on hooks, and the stone staircase which seemed to spiral upwards as in a lighthouse. The walls in the vestibule were lined with small wooden boxes, many of which had shoes and sandals of all descriptions in them. As they were drying their feet, Sarah explained.

"Of course, washing one's feet is purely symbolic. We haven't actually got any feet and there is no dust to wash off them if we did have, but a large proportion of the students in the world are Asian, and they wash their feet before entering a house on the Surface, so they expect to do it here as well.

"It is a good example of things that people don't have to do but choose to because they have always done it".

"I don't mind, I think it's a rather nice custom. The number of times people have traipsed mud through our cottage! I wish we had a footbath".

"Yes, I like it too. Of course, if we didn't want to take part we could have just imagined it wasn't there and clomped upstairs in hobnail boots, but this sets the tone better, I think".

"Yes, it feels like being in a public library".

"Come on, up we go". The staircase, which had looked very narrow, was suddenly wide enough for them to walk side by side, so William fell in beside her.

"Something you just said, Sarah, sounds a bit odd to me. You just said that a large proportion of the students are Asian. What, in Wales?"

"Well, I can't speak for really far back in history, but traders from the Middle East sailed to Wales and Cornwall. They would have washed their feet. It is said that Jesus came here with his uncle Joseph of Arimathea, and Jesus washed feet. The Romans were here and the soldiers would have bathed their feet after a long march, and there are a lot of Indians and Pakistanis here now. On top of that, there are Buddhist colonies in Wales

"So, there is quite a tradition of foot-bathing in Wales. However, it isn't only that really. There are a lot of visiting teachers and students. Transportation is no problem, so some people choose to study all over the world, all over the Universe for that matter".

"What? You have students from Outer Space here under our mountains?"

"Yes", she said laughing "and teachers. Why wouldn't we have?"

"Is that the source of UFO sightings?"

"Oh, I wouldn't have thought so… People project themselves, they don't use space ships, but it is possible that they might imagine one for a laugh and cloak themselves in that".

"But that would be deceiving millions of people. It doesn't sound like very fitting behaviour for religious students to me".

"No, it probably doesn't, but students will be students. You know what they are like… Always up for a laugh, and where's the harm? Anyway, I am not saying that they are responsible for the sightings, just that there are a few of them that I wouldn't put it past… Teachers as well for that matter… Anyway, we don't think of ourselves as religious students, more students of life and natural phenomena".

"That does sound less stuffy and monastic".

"Good, because while we do take our studies seriously, we are not all killjoys".

"Where are all the classrooms in this school? We've been walking for a while now, and I haven't seen one. You certainly try to tire your students out here before they get to their lessons, don't you?"

"Pardon? You are not tired are you?"

"No, I'm not now that you mention it, but I think that I ought to be. This staircase is very steep".

"It doesn't have to be, but it is how we like it, and we have passed hundreds of classrooms, as you call them. Pick one".

He looked from Sarah's beguilingly radiant face to the external wall of the tower and saw a wooden door on every other step that he had somehow overlooked previously.

"I've been so engrossed talking to you, my dear, that I hadn't noticed all these doors. That is unbelievable! We must have passed a hundred".

"Many, many more, William… all missed opportunities to learn because we were distracted from our true objective".

"Can we go into one and look around?"

"Certainly, take your pick".

"No, I don't like to. I don't want to disturb a class in progress… You look, make sure it's clear".

"No, you have to choose. I make my own choices every day, and you have to make yours".

"How about this one?" he asked a few steps further up. He put his ear to the door. "I can't hear anyone; I think this one is empty".

"Try".

He listened again, tapped the door and gingerly pushed down on the handle. To his surprise, it opened easily. He left it ajar and turned to beckon Sarah. For some reason he had been expecting rusty hinges and swollen timber. She stepped closer, but as he went to push on the door to go in, it swung open as if on its own to reveal a large, bearded man, who was apparently in his late fifties. William was horrified.

"I'm sorry", he stammered "I though that this room was empty. I didn't mean to disturb you".

"You haven't disturbed me, William. Hello, Sarah, nice to see you again. Come in both, please".

William turned to look at Sarah; he was shaking his head slightly in disbelief.

"You seem surprised, William. I hope that I didn't startle you back there".

They were standing in the middle of a medium-sized classroom with dark wood panelling on three walls, and two arched windows cut into the fourth. There was no furniture on the polished wooden floorboards and only one small picture on each of the three panelled walls, but he couldn't make them out

"Er, no, sorry, it was my fault for disturbing you, but how do you know my name?"

"Don't you recognise me? Have you never seen me before?"

William studied the craggy, old face and his bright hazel eyes. There was something familiar about him, but William could not place him.

"Did we meet at one of the sheep farmers' markets, or somewhere like that? Are you a farmer, I mean, were you?" He looked to Sarah for help.

"You can say 'are' or 'were', it doesn't bother me, but the answer is the same. No, I was a fisherman. Last time around, I had a little fishing boat off St. David's in Pembroke, but that was a while ago now.

William held his chin and shook his head. "No, sorry. I can't remember meeting no fisherman from Pembroke. I think I've only been there once. On our honeymoon, Sarah, forty-five years ago. You would only have been a toddler then.

"What's your name if you don't mind me asking?"

"John", he said laughing. "Excuse me, but you might think I'm fifty-ish, but I haven't walked the Surface in a body for nigh on two hundred years. Oh, dear me, no! I didn't mean that you might have seen me on the beach in Pembroke".

"You've lost me, John. I don't understand, sorry".

"No, well that's fair enough. That's why you came to our school and that is why you knocked on my door. Let's sit down. Floor or chairs?"

John and Sarah exchanged glances.

"Chairs, I think", said John. "Pull up those two chairs and we'll have a nice little chat".

William looked behind him to where John had pointed and pulled up a chair and when he sat on it there was a table with Sarah sitting next to him and John opposite.

"It's like this, William. I am what we call your Spirit Guide… or one of them anyway".

"Sarah mentioned Spirit Guides this afternoon. I wondered if I would ever meet mine, er, you".

"In fact, we have met many times, but you either didn't notice me, ignored me or forgot about me when you woke up".

"I apologise if I was rude".

"It's an occupational hazard, don't worry about it. You weren't purposely rude. I stood with you on Jones' Peak many times when you had your sheep and tried to keep you company, but perhaps you couldn't hear me, and more recently, since Sarah has been here, I have accompanied you on many of your walks with your dog and tried to console you. I have also tried to appear in your dreams and give you advice or sometimes just talk to you about the price of fish.

"From our point of view, it is difficult to know how much our charges hear or understand us. It can be very disheartening".

"I'm sure. Well, I will certainly be looking and listening out for you from now on, John. Can I ask you something?"

"Yes, certainly, that is the question I have been waiting for you to ask every day since you could speak".

"Why are you with me? Did you choose me, and if so why?"

"A lot of these sorts of choices are fairly automatic. I went through school as Sarah is doing now, and learned a lot about myself and my profession. In the course of doing that, you meet many people – you could call some of them case studies. Over time, you learn what sort of people you can best empathise with, and that allows you to make an informed choice.

"I selected you, partly because we led, or you would lead a similar life to the one I had. You were to become a shepherd, and I had been a fisherman in a rowing boat. Both people spend a lot of time on their own.

"I checked with you and my teachers, we were all in agreement, and so that was that. There wasn't really all that much to it, it was pretty automatic".

"How do you mean 'you checked with me'? I was only a baby".

"Not before you were born, you weren't. You were a handsome, strapping young man of about twenty-five in appearance. Did you know him back then, Sarah?"

"Yes, but not well. We had met three or four times, and we arranged to be born near each other, be friends and possibly get married, if we hit it off well. Which we did, didn't we, William".

"Yes, we did, but all this is news to me. Why didn't I know anything about it?"

"This is a school, and you sought a teacher. When the student is ready, the teacher will appear. Knock and the door shall be opened.

"Anyway, you did know about it at the time obviously. However, it is better that one does not remember these plans when one is living one's life, so it has been arranged that the shock of entering one's body removes all psychic or spiritual memories in the average person.

"Yogis and adepts train themselves to remember, but that is different. However, the shock treatment doesn't always work and then people remember past lives, but that is rare".

"So, I have been here before… strange, none of it looks familiar".

"No, William, it won't do and for several reasons. One: you have not passed over yet, so you are still working with your Earthly memories; two: you will need to either have had some training before you pass over, or be counselled after the event, which I believe Sarah is involved with these days; and three: Annwn can change depending on who is here, but especially over time. Sixty-five years is not long, but it is enough to change to some degree and coupled with your stunted memory, it is no surprise that you don't recognise anything".

The three of them sat at the table, and William sensed that the meeting would be at an end if he didn't have any questions. It was not like a school where a teacher has an agenda to inculcate into the students. This one was student led.

"So, if you came into my dreams, John, and I don't mean to cast any doubt on your assertion that you did, what sort of things would you tell me? Prophesies… things like that?"

"Like which horse is going to win the Derby? No, William, no, not me. I wouldn't have the faintest idea. Some others might though, and this is what I was alluding to earlier when I said that I am only one of your Guides, albeit the main one. Sometimes, you might need specialist help that I alone cannot provide, and so under those circumstances, I would ask my Guide help me to find an appropriate assistant – a specialist.

"And now my rôle in your dreams. That specialist may not be able or competent enough to approach you on the Surface, so I would help him or her to get into your dreams to help you through that medium. Or I might decide that the best way to advise you is to manipulate a dream, to tell you a story in one of your dreams that illustrates the point that I want to make.

"At other times, I personally am capable of sitting next to you in a pub or walking next to you down the street".

William looked at Sarah who was gazing back at him excitedly, nodding her head.

"He can, William. John is very adept. That is hard to pull off. It's why I only appear to you in the cottage. It's because I can't hold the image for long, I keep shimmering or even disappearing like you said. In public, someone would be bound to notice. The shock could kill somebody. We have to be very careful of not hurting anyone".

"You are getting there, Sarah. Sarah is one of our best students, William. You are a very lucky man to have her on your side".

"Thank you, John. I have always been very proud of her".

She beamed and blushed and then looked down at her hands as she fought the impulse to feel pride.

"How can I distinguish between junk dreams and the meaningful ones, then, John?"

"A lot of students have a problem with this, William, but the solution is really quite a simple one. The fist thing I would say though, is that there is no such thing as a junk dream, as you put it. Dreams that might seem nonsensical upon awakening might just be your mind filing away things that have happened to you recently.

"I don't just mean events that you are aware of like your shoelace coming undone or losing your glasses, but also other things like my having tried to communicate with you or your stomach producing too much acid. There are many things going on in your body and indeed your life that you know nothing about, yet your mind will record them all faithfully in deep storage.

"This happens very quickly like your computers, but faster still, and you only see a blur, if anything, so you try to make something of it. These dreams do not remain in the memory for long, because your mind knows that they are not worth remembering.

"These are the dreams that you have forgotten before you sit down for your breakfast. Be thankful that they are not going to clutter your day.

"Then there are the dreams that you remember at breakfast and tell your spouse about. You go to work and you can still remember them. You may try to analyse them or tell a colleague at work. These are the important ones, and a wise student will collect them in a book.

"Do you see how the dreams are sorted automatically again? Just as I said earlier about many things in real life?"

"Real life? What is unreal life?"

"I use the term to distinguish between life, which is important – the one that goes on forever no matter what, and the temporary life on the Surface which people spend so much time agonising over.

"Temporary things are not real and so unimportant. These are things such as status, wealth, car, boat, beautiful spouse, holidays abroad, second home, even physical condition et cetera, as opposed to permanent things, which are real such as your character, reputation and your Spiritual achievement and education, which affect your Karma, which affects the entirety of your infinite existence.

"We have all chased these temporary status symbols in at least one life, in many for most of us, but even after centuries of countless lives, many people are still running around in their wheel like hamsters, while those who have realised their error, soar like eagles".

"I have so much that I want to ask you, John, because every time you answer one of my questions another two or three occur to me".

"I know the feeling, William", he replied laughing. "All the best students say that, don't they, Sarah?" She blushed again.

"You have to know how fast you can go though. You have to learn how quickly your Self can assimilate and operate with the knowledge that you are acquiring. It does not matter in the slightest whether that is lightening fast or at a snail's pace, because you have all the time that exists to get where you are going. Does that make sense, William?"

"Yes, John. Will I remember any of this when I go back?"

"The truth is that I do not know. The chances are that you will remember very little, but it will be in deep storage, ready to be brought back at any time. The trick is finding the trigger that will bring the memories of discussions such as these back.

"Most people use meditation, contemplation or prayer, it's all the same really; some even use music. You will have to see what suits you".

"I think that we had better leave it there then for now, John, I don't want to take up too much of your time, if I'm not going to remember any of this" he said sadly. "It's a shame though; I have never spent a happier hour in school in my whole childhood than this one. If you had been my teacher back then, I probably would have gone on to university".

"I appreciate the compliment, William, but you wouldn't have. You had already decided to become a shepherd before you were born".

They both stood up laughing. John made the Namaste and William copied him. The table and the chairs disappeared and John walked them to the door.

"Until we meet again", they said and William and Sarah left pulling the door shut behind him. At the last moment, he opened the door again to say something, but the room was empty.

"He's gone", said William rather forlornly.

"He's never far away from you, Willy. You only ever have to think of him and he will come to you. He is your special friend and he will never let you down. Remember that, no matter what happens to you throughout your life. He will not abandon you until you get back here and tell him that you no longer need him".

"I can't imagine that ever happening. You and he are the most amazing people I have ever met".

They started their descent, but after rounding one corner, the door was before them and there was no footbath. William looked at Sarah.

Anticipating his questions, she said, "Who wants to waste time walking down stairs and who washes their feet before they go outside?"

He smiled, shrugged and slipped his feet into his sandals.

"Now I remember where else I've heard of Annwn. The Hounds of Annwn, Cŵn Annwn! I knew the name sounded familiar. The Hounds of Annwn, the Hounds of Hell, we were told the story in school, do you remember?"

"Yes", she said laughing. "Old Mrs. Taylor read it to us for Halloween one year and we were all too frightened to walk home!"

"Do they exist, the hounds, I mean?"

"Oh, yes! Would you like to see them?"

"Er, yes, all right, are they penned up?"

"If you want them to be, but why would you? Oh, the story, of course! Like most of those old stories, there is only a grain of truth in it. You, and everyone else, are immortal. All right? Nothing can hurt you but ignorance and that will be your own fault either for not paying attention to your Spirit Guide or not thinking for yourself. Nobody else can hurt you unless you let them and the same goes for scary monsters and vicious dogs. I'll show you the hounds now".

They stepped outside the tower and Sarah looked about herself.

"This way..." she said.

A Night in Annwn

6. WALKABOUT

To the right of the huge open gates of Annwn was a small wooden arched door with a glassless window in it. Sarah peered inside. "Oh, that's a shame, they have gone out", she sighed. "Still, I can show you their kennel". She opened the door and they went in. The stonewalled chamber was the size of a large modern living room and had a layer of straw on the stone floor. The portcullis in the font wall was raised to let the dogs out and await their return.

"They spend a lot of time running about all over the countryside", explained Sarah,

"How many are there?" asked William.

"A dozen, I think".

"Not a bad size room for a dozen dogs, is it?" opined William.

"No, it's a nice size, but then space isn't a problem here and these dogs are not your ordinary dogs. They are large. The smallest, Annie, is about the size of an Irish wolfhound and the largest, Bob and Harry, are like Shetland ponies.

"Annie, Bob and Harry? They are not very scary names for the Hounds of Hell, are they?"

"But they aren't scary… not in the least! They are the sweetest, most adorable, loving animals. I have told you already that there is nothing in Annwn to be frightened of. Nobody and nothing can hurt you except yourself.

"I know about the legends on the Surface, but they are just silly stories made up by silly people to frighten other people silly enough to believe them. Look, if you own an expensive flock of sheep or herd of cattle, what is the best way to protect them? Hire expensive guards to watch over them all day and all night, or put a pound in the vicar's collection tray and ask him to tell everyone blood-curdling tales about vicious hounds from Hell and be done with poachers for ever?

"It really is a no-brainer, isn't it?" Let's go for a walk, maybe we will come across them". They walked under the portcullis into a field of grass. "Have you noticed anything?" she asked looking back at the castle. William turned to look at it as well "Tell me what you see".

"Er, a medieval castle… it looks a bit like Camelot in the film. A pennant on that tower, er, bright sun, blue sky, a few cumulus clouds. It looks like it will be a nice afternoon. What am I supposed to be seeing?"

"Oh, you are not supposed to be seeing anything, but we just came out of that gate and walked across the moat and there is no bridge, and if we are underground, how come there is sun, sky and clouds?"

"Oh, yes! Funny, isn't it?"

"Yes, it keeps me smiling; especially when I think about life on the Surface. I'm glad you think so as well".

"This is like being in a dream, isn't it? You can be looking at something, then you look away and look back and it has changed, but you can't always remember what has changed and how. Is that tower the school we just came out of?"

"Yes, the one with the flag".

"When we were walking up it, the stairs were about five feet wide, and the walls, judging by the window reveals, were a foot thick. So that makes the tower about twelve to fifteen feet wide, which that one is. But the room we were is was twenty feet by twelve, which means that the tower would have to be fifty-five to sixty feet wide, which that one clearly is not".

"That might be the logic on the Surface, but it does not apply here. It takes a bit of getting used to. There is a way of letting the scenery suggest itself to you, and once you have learned how to accept that, it doesn't change so much. It also helps if you have seen it before. The more often you go somewhere, the less it changes to suit your imagination, unless you force it too of course and you can do that at any time.

"It will change for you, because you have never been here before and so have no pre-conceived idea of what it is like, or should be like, or projects itself as".

"How can scenery 'project itself'? It doesn't seem to make sense".

"Perhaps it is just my bad choice of words. When you see an object on the Surface, you are seeing a reflection of light from it. You are not actually seeing the object itself, right?"

"I think so…"

"That is why people can argue about colours, because not all eyes perceive light in the same way, so the same item can appear different to different people. However, here, we don't need light to see, and, despite appearances, we haven't even got any functioning eyes. We see by impression, vibration, projection. We sense things more than see them.

"So, if a lot of people look at something, they will leave behind an impression of what they saw. There might be as many impressions as people who have seen it, but there will be a consensus of opinion, and that is what I mean by allowing the image to project itself. In that way, you will be seeing the average of what everyone who saw it before you has seen. Or you can refocus and look at it yourself as if for the first time, er, make your own image. It is completely up to you, as everything always is".

"It's a whole new world, isn't it?"

"Well, no, not really. Spirit, er, we were around long, long before the Earth was formed, so the Earth is the new world. This is the old world, where Spirit, er, we have always lived".

"And you say that there are millions of places like this?"

"I don't remember saying that. I didn't mean to anyway. The truth is that everywhere is like this… not exactly like this with a castle, moat and fields, but everywhere works according to the same rules. So, you could say that there are millions of places like this, yes. That would be one way of looking at it, but would you go to the seashore and give every grain of sand its own individual name or number, or just call it a beach?

"It is entirely up to you".

"So, you believe that there is life on other planets too then?"

She stopped and looked at him. "It is not a question of belief… Unless of course you are the sort of person who says, 'I believe that two plus two equals four'. Personally, I would prefer to say that I know that they do, but then again, that is up to you, isn't it? It is your choice".

"Where are we going, Sarah?"

"Somewhere and nowhere, we are just walking and talking. If you are bored with walking, we could fly, if you want".

"What? Imagine a helicopter and pilot, eh?"

"That would be one method of doing it, but it was not what I had in mind…"

"Don't tell me! Imagine that we are birds and flap our way over there?"

"No, but that is possible as well".

"Become rockets?"

"Now you are being silly. No, just imagine that you are where you want to be. See those two mountains over there. I'll race you to the top of the one on the left".

"That's not fair! I don't know how to do it".

"It's easy. Just imagine that you are standing on the top of that mountain and will yourself to be there". William disappeared and Sarah followed him.

"You cheated!" she exclaimed, "You didn't say 'Ready, steady, go!'"

"It was a bit of a shock to me too to find myself standing up here all alone, I can tell you. It was exhilarating though. What a rush! That beats three pints of beer and a packet of crisps any day. And those guys in the pub don't know that they can do that?"

"I doubt it. They may never even have been home. I think they just sit in the pub all day talking and drinking. I don't watch them all the time. Most of us lose patience with people like that".

"Race you to the other peak over there. Ready, steady, go! Dead heat! So, why doesn't someone tell them?"

"Oh, many people have tried! I have even had a go myself".

"What's the problem, won't they listen?"

"Let's put it this way. You and Dai are sitting in the Teg one Saturday afternoon, watching a rugby international, playing Crib and having a pint, when a young woman comes in, a stranger, and says, 'Don't your realise that there is more to life than sitting here? Come with me; let me show you how to really enjoy yourselves!' What would your reaction be?"

"I'd think you were a raving nymphomaniac who had just escaped from an asylum".

"So did they. It was one of my first assignments, and I admit that I could have handled it better, but men and other women met with the same sort of response. People just think that you're some kind of a nutter - a religious fanatic usually, like a Mormon or someone from the Salvation Army".

"Yes, I can see that they might. Hey, it does happen though, doesn't it?! Are you saying that some of the religious nutters that I have met in pubs could have been ghosts?"

"No, I wasn't, but it is true that they could have been. Doing that sort of work is one of the top jobs - most important tasks, I should have said. There are a few of them".

"Really? Spreading the 'Word' like the Hari Krishnas?"

"I knew you would say something like that. The higher tasks are the relief of suffering and the eradication of ignorance in all forms of life'.

"You try to stop people crushing beetles too?"

"Are you trying to rile me, Willy, because you will not succeed, but I will resent your trying to?"

"I'm sorry, Sarah. I was only having a bit of sport with you".

"Times and places come to mind. Since you brought it up, I do prefer people not to kill other creatures especially in a cruel or sadistic way. However, I was talking primarily about the higher orders of life especially mammals, but it applies to all animals really, fish, plants and trees, if you want to stretch it that far. Some do, most don't".

"So, tell me, what would you be doing if I were not here to distract you?"

"Any of a number of things. I started my training comforting abused, abandoned and suffering animals like poor Kiddy..."

"Hey, that is not fair!"

"Yes, it is! Then I moved on to people who are suffering like the morally bankrupt and the bereaved like you. Before you ask, no, that is not why I was at our cottage. I was there because I love you and the dog..."

"I have been meaning to ask, where is she?"

"I don't know. Try calling her".

"I'd feel stupid calling a dog on the top of a deserted mountain".

"You don't need to shout, you haven't got a voice box anyway, just call her as you normally would, but in your head. Use telepathy".

He gave her a look that for a second questioned whether she was joking, but a second later, Kiddy was between them wagging her tail.

"Wow! What a girl, both of you. I won't ever doubt you again, Sarah. I hadn't thought about us not being able to have voices either. But wait a moment, you move your lips when you talk, and so did those men in the pub".

"Yes, I do it for your benefit, and the drinkers do it because they don't know any better, but it is completely unnecessary".

"So, where do you go from comforting the bereaved".

"It's not like a four-year course at university. It's an on going project. I still comfort suffering animals, it is not beneath me and never will be and there is a great deal of work to do with those who either don't realise that they have passed over, or can't believe their eyes because it is not like they were expecting, but I want to become a Spirit Guide, like John.

"That is what my training is leading up to. Just before you collapsed, I was on a battlefield in Syria. One battle or sometimes even just one bomb can leave hundreds of people wandering around not realising that they have passed on. They often become dreadfully distraught. They can't understand why their friends and family can't see them or won't answer them when they try to talk to them.

"It is pitiful... heartbreaking. At least the blokes in the pub are happy in their ignorance. Millions more are not.

"Just imagine the work that had to be done in the First World War battlefields, or in Nagasaki and Hiroshima in the Second World War! That amount of anguish can linger for a very long time. In fact, it is another example of a lot of people imprinting a place with an image or atmosphere. It is the same sort of thing I was talking about earlier".

"Yes, I understand. They say that still nothing will grow in some parts of Belgium and France because of the amount of sorrow that was poured out there in a very short period of time. Others say it's just the chemicals from the weapons".

"It could be both, but I can tell you that the atmosphere on a battlefield when it is over is horrendous - even a small one".

"I can see that it shook you up, my dear. Can we go down to our rock on our hill now, please".

"Certainly. Tell Kiddy to stay here. You can call her in a few seconds".

And a few seconds later, the three of them were sitting on their love rock a little way up from their cottage.

"It's just like the good old days, sitting here with you like this, Sarah. I have missed you so".

"I know, and I have missed you too. It was hard in the beginning to be so near to you and see and feel your pain, but not be able to do anything about it".

"What will happen next?"

"I don't know, my dear, nobody knows what another has planned for the future. Most of us don't even know what is in store for ourselves. You have to be well advanced to know that. It is still out of my league. However, I assume that your body will recover - that is what they said, right? When that happens you will have to go back to it".

"But will I be able to come back here to visit you before I pass over?"

"There is a chance, but I don't know how big it is. We have many visitors from the Surface, but they have been aware for a long time and practiced regularly. You are starting from square one, but you do know that Annwn exists, so that is an advantage. Many still have to learn that. I can come to you though, and now that you will be certain that it is me, I can come in this form, so no more shimmering and disappearing.

"What will become of us, Sarah? I don't want to go back. I want to stay here with you…"

"Please, Willy, don't talk like that… You chose to be born in a certain place and with certain people because that environment was the best you could find to teach you the lessons you wanted to learn. It is a long and hard road to get where you are today, do not even consider giving up before your journey is at an end. Nothing is worth that. Be patient, have courage and see your life out. Annwn will always be here and you can rest assured that I will be waiting for and watching out for you. He wanted to take her hand, but knew that he could not and he wondered whether he was able to cry.

"Do you visit any of our old friends, Sarah, and can they see you?"

"No, I used to visit Joan and Mary, and I thought that Rose might be able to see me, but none of them ever reacted, so I gave up after a while".

"How about other ghosts, for want of a better word".

"We tend to say 'people in Spirit' but it's a bit of a mouthful. I don't mind the word ghost, but I know that some do object. I talk to others like me all day. Why do you ask?"

"Oh, it's just that I haven't seen you speak to anyone except John since I've been here".

"No, well, you wouldn't notice me talking to anyone if I don't move my lips, but people are very sensitive. They know we were married, and know that you are only visiting, so they are giving us some space, that's all. They are just being nice. Would you like to meet some of the others?"

"No, not necessarily. I was just wondering, that's all. So, you have your circle of friends here then?"

"Oh, yes. There are people from school, and people I have met through them and the teachers. You know, all sorts really..."

"And is there anyone special?"

"Everyone is special in their own way, aren't they?"

"Yes, but you are a beautiful young woman again, I am sure that men find you attractive..."

"I hope they do, but our wedding vows were 'till death us do part', weren't they?"

"Yes, I just heard you say 'we were married'. It got me thinking..."

"You are a silly Billy aren't you? I don't believe in death. I am only pulling your leg. There is no-one else, and never has been. I love you, and that is why I came to the cottage to see how you were.

"Willy, can you hear that?"

"A pack of dogs. It's the hunt probably".

"What, the people in pink?"

"Yes, the county hunt…"

"Get away with you. I'd know that sound anywhere. They are my babies. They are the Hounds of Annwn".

"Will they come if you call them? I'd love to see them".

"They might do. It depends how much fun they're having. They get so excited. I'll try". She put the tips of the thumb and forefinger of her right hand to her lips and blew. There was a piercing, undulating whistle".

"My God, you haven't forgotten how to call dogs then!"

"No", she laughed. "Here they come. Look!"

William followed her finger and could hardly believe his eyes.

"Jesus, Sarah! They aren't dogs, that is a herd of Welsh mountain ponies". Within seconds the hounds had surrounded Sarah and were vying for her attention

"Aren't they lovely? You're all my lovely boys and girls, and you too Kiddy. You're all very special to me"

William felt a twinge in his stomach and automatically put his hand to it. "Oh, Sarah, I think that pub grub was five hundred years old as well. It's making me feel peculiar".

"Is it like a tickling inside you?"

"Yes, what is it?"

"OK, boys and girls, move along now. Run off and play. I'll come to see you again later". They seemed to understand and ran off up to the hill howling raucously

"It's not the food for sure, William. Didn't I tell you that nothing here can hurt you? Someone is trying to revive your body and it is calling you back for assistance".

"But I don't want to go back right now, I want to stay here and talk with you. Can't you tell it to wait a couple of hours?"

"No, it doesn't work like that. While it is alive, it has first call on your time. It's like if your burglar alarm goes off, you go and see to it immediately".

"But this is intolerable! I have missed you for five years, then, when I find you again, my own body calls time on our meeting after a few hours".

"Come on, Willy, I'll go with you, but one way or another you have to go now. Say goodbye to Kiddy, and I'll send her home".

"Goodbye for the time being, girl. Come and visit me again, won't you?" he said and she was gone.

"OK, think about your body. I'll be right with you". A second later, they were standing in a hospital room looking down on his body. His chest was bare and a doctor was using a defibrillator on it. He felt another tickle as the doctor activated the device and his body jumped. He looked very poorly. Sarah motioned him towards his body.

"Just get into it like a sleeping bag", she urged.

"It feels like I wet the bed, it's all cold and damp", he said climbing in and pulling a face.

"Don't worry, it always feels like that, when you've been out of it for a while. Try to give them some encouragement".

William opened his eyes, and then his mouth but no words would come out.

"We have him, he's back! William, can you hear me. You're going to be all right. Just try to take it easy".

"William tried to speak again, but it was as if he had forgotten how to work the muscles, so he simply nodded and tried to stay awake, because suddenly he was feeling exhausted.

"You be a good Willy for the nice doctors and nurses, do you hear?" she said planting a kiss above his forehead. "I'm going outside to see how our daughter is".

As he watched Sarah walk through the wall to the corridor outside, he was already beginning to forget what had happened to him and where he had been.

"Try to stay awake for a little while, William. I want to hear you speak. You had us very worried about you, you know, but your daughter never gave up hope. No, siree, not for one second. How are you feeling?"

"Ti..." he heard himself say as if from a distance.

"Tired? A workhorse like you? I don't believe it. You've been asleep for a week! They say that too much sleep is bad for you, don't they, William. Try to stay awake for just a little while longer, and then we'll let you go to sleep. Your daughter is anxious to see you".

"OK, nurse, let's put all this apparatus away. We won't be needing it for William anymore today, will we, William? The nurse is going to clean you up a bit. She will help you look your best, while I go and put your daughter's mind at ease. Is there a message you want me to give her from you?"

"Yes, just say that her mother is with us".

"Sure, William, I'll tell her".

64

7. RE-REWAKENING

William was starting to drift off to sleep when his daughter entered the room. He could see how worried she was by her expression.

"How are you, Dad?"

"I'm all right, Becky; in fact, I am feeling stronger by the minute. It is good to see you again".

"We have all been so worried about you".

"I'm really sorry to have been such a nuisance..." He was searching his memory, "It was you who found me this morning, wasn't it?" He watched her looking around for advice. A nurse nodded.

"You think that you fell ill this morning, do you, Dad?"

"It is rather hazy, was it yesterday?" He saw Becky look at the nurse again.

"It was eight days ago, Dad..."

"No... Eight days? Really? But how can that be? I remember... I remember walking back from the Teg, and seeing Kiddy... Has she passed away?"

"Yes, Da. I know how much she meant to you. We all loved her very much, but she was very old. John buried her in the back garden of the cottage..."

"I have seen her since then, I think. I saw her half an hour ago with your mother. I could swear I did..."

"Yes, the doctor gave me your message..."

"Sarah said that she was going out to see how you were. Did you see her?"

"Er, I'm not certain, Dad..." she replied not sure what to say without upsetting him, "but I'm sure that Mum is here with us in your time of need. Is there anything I can get you?"

"No, thank you, Becky. It is my memory that I want back. I know that I am forgetting a lot, but I don't know how to retrieve those memories. I dreamed about your mother and Kiddy... and, er... No, it won't come... It is so frustrating. I have been dreaming for eight days, but my memory only accounts for ten minutes". He could see the concern in her eyes and it distressed him. "OK, Becky, don't worry about it now, but it was you who found me, wasn't it?"

"Yes, you remember that, eh?"

"I don't know... I think I was told, but maybe I was still partly conscious. But it must have been late at night, eh? Why did you come to check up on me? It was midnight or not?"

"Yes, but how do you know that?"

"How did you know that I was in trouble?"

"I don't know".

"And you don't think about it?"

"I have been thinking about nothing else for week. I had a bad dream... Mum was telling me that you were hurt and needed help. I didn't understand where you were, but I got in the car to drive to the cottage. I was nearly there and beginning to feel rather foolish, when I saw you slumped over something. It was you and Kiddy... I thought you were dead at first, but I called for an ambulance to meet us at the doctor's surgery.

"I thought that that was easier than trying to explain where we were. Then I checked you again. You had a pulse, and so I gave you all the assistance I could remember from the Girl Guides, bundled you into the car, and I will never know how I managed that, put Kiddy in the boot and took you to Doc Williams. Half an hour later, an ambulance arrived and brought you here.

"We have all been waiting for you to come around ever since. Oh, Da, I have been so worried..." She broke down in tears.

"It's all right, now, Becky. You saved my life. It was a miracle".

"Amen to that! It was a miracle to be sure. You look tired, Da, perhaps I should let you get some rest?"

"You didn't see your mother outside in the corridor then?"

"No, the doctor told me that you said she was here, but I assumed that that was you being, er, delusional, you know, after coming out of a coma".

"Maybe I was, Becky, I don't know any longer. Look, I am rather tired for a man who has been asleep for a week, so why don't you go home and get some sleep too? I appreciate your being here for me, but you look pretty worn out too".

"OK, Dad, if you are sure. What will you do?"

"Oh, just sleep. Don't worry about me now, I feel as if I could sleep for another week".

"Is there anything I can bring in for you?"

"No, my dear, not for now. I can't think of anything…"

∞

William dreamed that he was standing in a field before a great moated castle with a flag waving from a tower inside the walls. He thought that he could just make out a woman in one of the tower's windows. She was waving a handkerchief and shouting, but he couldn't quite understand what she was saying. He was thinking that she looked like a damsel in distress, when he heard a pack of baying hounds. They sounded as if they were hunting, and he didn't want to get in their way in case their bloodlust was up, so he hid behind a bush and watched.

The shaggy, grey hounds ran past him at a terrific speed with their mouths wide, showing their huge fangs; they were the biggest dogs he had ever seen! All except the last one who was struggling to keep up. It was a black Welsh sheepdog, and she slowed as she approached where William was hiding. She sniffed the air and looked at him, wagged her tail, and then ran on, seemingly trying to catch up with the pack, which was already at the moat.

They leaped the moat without stopping, straight into an open section of the castle wall. The sheepdog hesitated, then jumped in the moat and swam across into the arms of the damsel who was waiting for them. The woman, who looked like Sarah, helped the dog up the bank and they disappeared inside. When he came out of hiding and started to run towards the opening, a portcullis came down with a resounding thump.

"Sarah!" he cried, "It's me, I've come back! Let me in!"

He felt a hand on his shoulder and looked around.

"It's all right, William. It was only a dream. You are all right now. Drink this". She turned, picked up a beaker of water and pushed a buzzer.

The doctor arrived a few minutes later.

"William, do you mind if we have a little chat? Are you feeling up to it?"

"I'm fine doctor, that 'forty winks' – a power nap - them yuppies calls it now, isn't it? – did me a power of good". He laughed at his own joke and the doctor smiled with him.

"Yes, very good, William. Good. Nurse, you can take a break if you like, I'll sit with William for a while. I'll buzz when we're through". He waited for her to leave the room before continuing. "Have you been dreaming a lot, William?"

"Yes, I have… a lot more than normal. Why, doctor?"

"Do these dreams disturb you?"

"No, I can't say that they do. Are they a side effect of all the drugs you've been pumping into me?".

"They could be, but I think that that is unlikely. You have been on standard treatments, and while most drugs can cause increased or decreased nocturnal… er, dreaming, more often they don't. Anyway, the dreams that they produce are often confused, even frightening, which is why I asked you".

"No, I haven't been having nightmares, if that's what you mean".

"Yes, that is what I mean. So what have you been dreaming about, if you don't mind my asking?"

"No, I don't mind. They haven't been kinky or mucky dreams", he chuckled. His face turned serious, "I've been dreaming about my dead wife, Sarah, and my dead dog, Kiddy. Why? Is that significant?"

"I don't know, is it?"

"I don't know, but I enjoyed them, all but the one I just had".

"Are the dreams located in your house, the one you shared as a family and why was this last one so different from the others, William?"

"No, they never took place at home, doctor. I can't remember too well, but I know that they were happy dreams. I think we were in a big castle. Anyway, I just saw a castle again, but this time my wife and my dog were 'away from me'. It's hard to explain… before, they were right by my side – I could reach out and almost touch them! Just like I'm doing to you now… But in this dream, they were away from me. They knew I was there, but they didn't come over, and I couldn't get to them either.

"That's what made this last one a little sad, but I was still pleased to see them though".

"That is interesting, William, very interesting. During the eight days you were in a coma, you sometimes talked. People used to call it babbling, but these days we pay more attention to it, especially in coma cases". He took a notebook out of his jacket and looked for a page. "You often said the words: Sarah, Kiddy, Annwn, castle, hounds and the pub. We know that Sarah was your wife, and Kiddy your dog… is there anything you can tell me about the other words?"

"Annwn is the Other World, and I just dreamed about a castle and dogs, or hounds, if you like, and the pub may be the Teg, the Bryn Teg in the village. I don't know".

"Yes, I chanced looking Annwn up on the Internet. Annwn is what you say, and there was a reference to the Hounds of Annwn. Did you know about them?"

"A teacher, Mrs Taylor, told us a story about them in Junior School. It frightened the bejesus out of us, but that is all".

"All right, William. We'll leave it at that for now. I would like you to have a chat about your dreams with a colleague of mine tomorrow, would that be all right?"

"A shrink?"

"No, a counsellor, but someone who is very interested in dreams".

"All right".

"Thank you, William. I'll see you tomorrow".

∞

"Hello, William. I hope that you are well this afternoon. I have brought the friend I was telling you about yesterday. William this is Sally James".

"Just call me Sally, William. Nice to meet you".

"Nice to meet you too, Sally".

"Dr. Mathews has been telling me about the dreams you have been having. They sound fascinating, would you mind talking to me about them as well?"

"No, not at all. What I can remember of them, but I think that the doctor knows more than I do. I was out for the count".

"Yes, so I understand, still you were actually there, so to speak, weren't you? Our man on the spot..."

"So, William, why don't we begin? You have no objection to my recording the sessions and making notes, do you?"

"No, Sally, you carry on".

"Thank you. Now then, first things first. I want you to relax and just tell me everything that you can remember, in any order that it comes to you. Can I get you a glass of water or anything?"

"No, I'm just fine, thanks... You're not going to hypnotise me, are you?"

"No, not if you don't want me to. Perhaps another time, if you want. Please begin in your own time".

William told her as much as he could remember about his 'dreams', which was a lot less than he thought could have filled eight days.

"I'm sorry, Sally, but doesn't sound enough to fill an afternoon, let alone a week".

"Don't worry about it, William. It is often the case. Perhaps, we can uncover more, if I ask you questions based on what you have just told me and the notes that Dr. Matthews and the nurses took. They are really only words and a few phrases".

"Whatever you say, Sally?"

Forty minutes later, William was feeling very frustrated with the interview. "I'm sorry, Sally, I just don't seem to be able to remember any more. I wish I could, believe you me!"

"Yes, I do, William. Look, why don't we call it a day. That has been an hour, and it is enough for now. You mentioned hypnosis earlier. I would like to try that tomorrow, if you have no objection".

"That's fine by me, I ain't never been hypnotized before".

"There is nothing to it. I'll see you tomorrow. Is the same time all right?"

"Any time is all right for me, ask the doctor".

"I'll do that, bye, William", she said smiling.

After tea, Becky arrived.

"How are you doing, Da?"

He told her that he was feeling well, and about his dreams.

"The doctor and a counsellor seem very interested in them. Why would that be, do you reckon?"

"Well, I don't know really, but I imagine that it is all to do with psychiatry and Freudian psychoanalysis... or perhaps they just have an interest in religious beliefs or dreams".

"You don't think that they think I'm tŵp then?"

"Oh, no. If they thought that you were crazy, they would have moved you to a different kind of hospital".

"Yes, I suppose so. I just didn't want to be giving them more rope to hang me with if they thought that I was tŵp".

"Sarah, er, sorry, I mean Becky, what do you think of all this stuff about dreams and seeing your mother. You said that you dreamed about her as well..."

"Yes, I'm sure that I did, Da. I'm sure of it, but it was the first time for me. I have wanted to see her so often, however, it never happened until that night... but am I glad that I did then!"

"Me too, Becky, me too, but why did it happen that time and not before?"

"What do you know about Spiritualism, Da?"

"Nothing, why?"

"Well, I have been talking to all sorts of people about what happened to you, and me, and some people say that it has to do with Spiritualism..."

"I don't know, I honestly don't know, but I am willing to find out. I'm stuck in here for the foreseeable as far as I know, so why don't you go to the public library and get us some books on this Spiritualism?

"There may be something to it, or it may be a load of old cod's wallop, but there's no harm in reading up on it, is there?"

"No, all right, Da, I'll do that and bring them in tomorrow".

∞

Three days later, William had read every book that his daughter had brought him, had been hypnotized and had deep discussions with Sally and Becky on Spiritualism, Eastern religions such as Hinduism and Buddhism, and about methods of communing with the dead. In one such discussion with Sally, she mentioned The Tibetan Book of The Dead, and he involuntarily said, "Sarah told me that they consider the word 'dead' their 'N word".

"Pardon, William?" she had asked. "How do you know that?"

"You know, I have no idea... It just came out of my mouth. Hearing it was as big a surprise to me as it was to you, I can assure you, Sally".

"I have a feeling that that was a significant moment, but I don't know why either. It is so unlikely that you would just come up with something like that - 'their 'N-word'. That is remarkable. Are you sure that you haven't read it somewhere?"

"No, I couldn't guarantee that, Sally, I have read so much over the last few days".

Sally picked up her Smartphone and typed into it.

"No, I can't find the expression on the Internet, not even on Google Books, which means that you probably either made it up, or someone said it to you. Which visitors have you had?"

"Only my daughter, her husband and hospital staff... and Sarah, if you believe that sort of thing..."

"Yes, and Sarah..."

∞

"Well, as you know, William, under hypnosis, it was clear that you believed that you spent time with Sarah and Kiddy in the mythological place called Annwn, but your recollections of Annwn are nothing like those in any books or stories. Not that that matters. In fact, it suggests that you did not read your 'experiences', which tends to give them more credence, as far as I am concerned. If your account had paralleled stories, it would have been rejected out of hand. However, this makes it difficult too, because your version is not verifiable either. In short, we are stuck between the ship and the quay... on a rising tide".

That night, William started to practise some of the meditation techniques that he had been reading about. He did not expect any results, and he didn't achieve any, except a feeling of peace, which in turn helped him get another restful night's sleep, during which he dreamed of Sarah and Kiddy, but that was no longer unusual. Nor was having a barrier between them, unfortunately, but at least he had read one writer's reason for it and it made sense to him.

The reason for the separation was that he had not passed over. His body was now firmly planted on terra firma, so he could not cross over the divide between here and there, no matter what form it took. In William's case, the divide usually took the form of water - a moat or a stream.

He rationalized that for him to have been closer to Sarah before, he must have been on the very verge of giving up the ghost.

Two days later and William was deemed fit to be able to return home, so long as Becky organized that someone visited him every day. He also promised to get a mobile phone, and social services were alerted to his condition. He was glad to be going home, even though he had enjoyed his time in hospital, the conscious and unconscious times.

∞

When he walked into his cottage, assisted by Becky and her husband, John, he could not believe his eyes. They had completely redecorated the whole house.

"The place hasn't looked this good since your dear old Mum passed over!" he declared with a big smile that he would have been incapable of before his heart attack and stroke. I'm glad that you kept to the original colour scheme though, that was your mother's".

"I know, Da, I would never have changed that without your consent".

"I know, my dear, you are a good girl and always have been. Can you smell anything?"

They took a deep sniff. "Paint?" asked John.

"Yes, but underlying that?"

They tried again without success.

"Kiddy. I can smell Kiddy..."

"We did everything we could to wash the place out, William. We had the whole house cleaned professionally" objected John.

"I know that, John, I'm not having a pop. You could never get rid of the smell of Kiddy, because she is still here. And if Kiddy is here, then there is an odds-on chance that Sarah is as well".

William watched John closely for his reaction. He already knew that Becky believed, but he sensed that she didn't like to open up in front of her husband, and probably because he was sceptical or worse. He decided to try to help his daughter.

"I sense that you are not convinced of the Afterlife, John..."

"I'm not sure, no, William. I believe in God, Jesus and Heaven and all that, but I'm not sure about Annwn. It's just a Welsh fairy story".

William had no answer to that.

"You could well be right, John, but as the great English bard once said, 'A rose is just a rose by any other name'. Surely, it doesn't matter what name we call the place? 'Heaven' is an English word. Other people who use other languages don't call it Heaven, they have their own word for it. It is the concept that is important, not the word. It doesn't matter what number a house has, it matters whether it is a nice place to live. Do you follow me?"

"Yes, William", was all he could manage before his face crumpled and he began to cry. Becky put her arm around him and apologised to her father with a look. William said that it didn't matter in a similar manner.

He sat in his favourite seat at the table in the window and gazed out at the hill than rose before him. He knew that Sarah and Kiddy were there, but the circumstances were not right for them to be able to appear, because they would not want to frighten John. He had no problem with that. He could wait. He knew that they were there and that was good enough for now, but he knew that things would be different when he was alone... or the only Surface-dweller in the house.

8. BRYN TEG COTTAGE

Later that evening, when he had convinced his daughter and son-in-law that he was capable of taking care of himself, and that he knew how to use the new mobile phone that they had brought him and they had gone home, he moved from the seat to his armchair, which was opposite the one Sarah had used. As the natural light diminished, he did not augment it, and soon he was sitting in the dark, but all the while staring at her favourite chair and willing to speak to her or at least see her.

"Willy..." came into his mind all of a sudden and an image of Sarah, as if there were bad reception.

"Hello, beloved", he said, "I have missed you. Are you well?"

"Oh, nothing can hurt me here, unless I let it, but it has been very frustrating trying to keep in touch. I thought that once you had been here it would be a lot easier, but..."

"Don't worry about that, Sarah. We are both learning, aren't we?"

"Yes, surely, my husband and that will never stop for either of us now, because progress through the Spirit World is addictive. Once you realize what is possible, you want to achieve it, and when you have seen that, other possibilities appear... Just as you said in Annwn, my dearest. Some people say that once Spirit has got you, it will never let you go, but this is a backward way of expressing the phenomenon. When people realise what they are capable of, they want to progress. Like a good steeplechaser relishes getting to the next jump.

"You and I are racehorses, Willy, although it took us all our lives on the Surface to realise it. In that respect, you have seen the way before I did".

William tried a technique that he had read about. He 'unfocused his eyes' by looking at the space just behind where Sarah was attempting to appear, in the same way that a boxer aims his punch at the space just behind his opponent's head in order to achieve the maximum effect.

It helped, just as the book had said that it would. Memories came flooding back and that encouraged him to proceed.

"I can see you better now, Sarah".

"Good", he heard in his head, despite seeing her lips move. "I was talking to John, your Guide, he sends his best wishes by the way, and he suggested that we increase the chances of you knowing that I am near by using smell and sound..."

"It sounds good to me, anything that you or John suggest is good. How do we go about it?"

"Do you remember that time we went to Caldy Island?"

"Yes, on our honeymoon..."

"Yes, and you bought me perfume, talc and everything called Wild Gorse?"

"Yes, there is still some on your dressing table".

"Yes, I know. Well, I will bring that smell with me whenever I come to see anyone on the Surface. Please tell Becky. Another thing that I will do, is flick the light bulb – ping it. So you have several ways of knowing that I am nearby".

"Those are great ideas, Sarah. Will you use them outside this cottage as well?"

"Yes, John has shown me how to do these things anywhere".

"Sarah, as you probably know, I have been reading a lot about Spiritualism and Eastern religions lately, and I want to try some of the things they talk about. You know, like meditation, seeing and talking to Spirits, automatic writing and Astral travelling, but there are often warnings that bad things can happen to you unless you ask for permission from your Guardian – the one who protects the entrance at the base of the spine where the Kundalini lives. Is that Guardian John?"

"Yes, I know about your study interests, I help Becky choose the right books for you to read, although she doesn't know that yet. As far as the other things go, let me remind you that you are already seeing and talking to Spirit – me! But joking aside, you should direct all your queries, problems and the like to John. That doesn't mean that we can't discuss them, of course we can, but he is your mentor and one of mine too.

"I imagine that he will often be the Guardian you speak of, but he may also ask someone else to do the job, if he feels it appropriate".

"So, how do I do that?"

"It's the easiest thing in the world. Just sit or lie quietly and think his name, then ask your question. If you are seeking permission for what you might call a séance though, try to give him some notice. Say, three days, and if you plan to do it regularly, try to make it the same time and day each week. We attend a lot of meetings, or Circles, at Spiritualist churches, and others up and down the country and even all over the world

"A word of warning though, never try to contact anyone but me or John without having sought the proper permission, will you?"

"I have read that it can allow mischievous Spirits into your head".

"Yes, there are many thousands of Surface people who get hold of a Ouija board for a laugh and end up twp after a few sessions, because foolish Spirits have learned about their unprotected activities and go to make mischief. Often these people are diagnosed as schizophrenic and live most of the rest of their lives in institutions on strong drugs to suppress the two spirits battling for control of the one body".

"Sarah, could you remind me what happened when I was in that coma, I can't seem to remember".

"Slipping back into your body does that. I did tell you that it probably would. Anyway, we took you to Annwn, while Becky took your body to the doctor's…" She recounted the whole story, and that he had been so exhausted that he had slept there for a long while before coming around. "Does that ring any bells?"

"Yes, sort of. It's like déjà vu. As you were telling me the story, I would think 'Oh!, I remember that now!', it still doesn't seem enough to fill eight days though".

"Perhaps not, but that is what we did, and you were there for eight days. It is just that time is not the same here and there. Don't worry about it. I have a suggestion.

"Becky thinks about Spiritual matters often. This episode has awoken an interest in her as well as yourself, so I would like you to invite her to join your classes, your learning, or Development Circle, if you like".

"Certainly, I would like that very much. Will you and John be there too?"

"Yes, I will be there whenever I can. That is why it is best to give us regular times and dates, so that we can work you in. After a while, your meetings will become fixtures and other events will have to be fitted in around yours. However, I am one hundred percent positive that John will always attend your Circle meetings, and so will Becky's Spirit Guide. So that will make five of us and Kiddy…" she added as Kiddy walked in through the wall wagging her tail. William could see her, and tried to call her to him, but she sat by the side of Sarah's armchair.

"She can't come to you, not completely, William".

"No, I had forgotten. There's my lovely girl, Kiddy. I wish I could give you a biscuit. You are looking well, both of you are and I am so pleased to see you again. I have missed you".

"We have never been far away, and never ever will be, but I know what you mean".

∞

William started doing yoga exercises twice a day: in the morning before breakfast, and an hour before he wanted to go to bed. At first, he found the asanas difficult, but after a week or so, he actually looked forward to his sessions and added another thirty minutes: fifteen minutes of asanas and fifteen minutes of breathing exercises.

He still enjoyed a bottle of beer, but found some of the asanas impossible with a bloated belly full of beer, so he had to choose which one he wanted the more. The exercises won easily, and his consumption of alcohol diminished remarkably. The effect of this and the exercises was to cause him to lose weight, which relieved pressure on his back, knees and feet, making him feel younger, nimble and sprightly. He told his daughter that he felt twenty years younger.

"You look it too, Da, but it is not only your appearance; it is your attitude as well. You get up in the morning because you want to, not just to go to the bathroom or have lunch; you are excited and animated. You look and behave twenty years younger. You are even doing housework… for the first time in your life. I didn't think you even knew where the Hoover was kept.

"If you don't mind me saying so, you were becoming a bit of a drunken, old slob".

"Hey! That's no way to talk to your father, even if you are right. Lying in bed all morning, eating only fry-ups and drinking beer all day, was probably why I had that heart attack. And my aching back and knees and swollen feet are a thing of the past too. I do feel like a new man".

"You look great, Da. I was worried that you would slip into your old ways, when you came home, especially now that you haven't got Kiddy to take care of. I was thinking of getting you a puppy…"

"Oh, no, love. I couldn't be doing with puppy-training now…"

"Fair enough. I don't think you need a distraction anyway. You've got enough to occupy your mind, haven't you? I'm going to take up yoga as well. If it can do that for you in a fortnight, I want some of it too".

"You won't regret it, but it is tough in the beginning. The first week, say, but after that, you can see and feel the results and you want more.

"Look, I was talking to your mother a while back, and she suggested that I ask you if you want to practice meditation with me. I have been having séances every night since I came out of hospital, and am getting on quite well. I would have asked you earlier, but I wanted to learn a bit myself first. What do you say?"

"You really believe that you sit and talk to Mum, don't you?"

"Yes, but not only talk. I can see her as clearly as I can see you now. And not only your mother neither. I can see John, my Spirit Guide and Kiddy too".

She scrutinised his face as she always did when he talked like this, looking for signs of madness or mirth, but she had never discerned either.

"Yes, all right. I would like that. When?"

"Up to you. I do it every night, so pick an evening, but you have to stick to it, like bingo – same time, same night every week".

"How long for?"

"Up to you again – an hour, two hours, whatever you like".

"OK, but I'll have to sort out a time with John… my John".

"All right, no problem. Give me a call, but try to give me at least a day's notice".

She agreed, assuming that he wanted to prepare sandwiches or get something in.

∞

Becky arrived at twenty-five past six on the following Monday, tapped the open back door and walked straight in. "Dad! I'm here".

"Come on through, love. How are you doing? Take a seat at the table opposite me".

"Aren't we going to sit on the floor or in the garden on the grass? I've got my leotard and tights on underneath, I bought them specially on Saturday".

"No, this will do nicely. You can keep the training gear for your yoga. Those books are for you, don't say I never buy you nothing" he chuckled.

"What are they?" she asked laying the two books side by side.

"There's one on yoga and one on Spiritual training techniques. Your mother recommended them and I got Dai to ask his daughter to order them on line. Amazon Woman or River… Amazon something or other anyway. I bought two of each, so we both got one.

"You can do the yoga at home and we'll do the exercises in the other one here. We will start chapter one tonight. It teaches safety and basic meditation techniques".

William taught her everything that Sarah and John had told him about the subjects and a lot of it was in the 'textbook', but not all. When there was only fifteen minutes of their allotted ninety left, they touched hands across the table and tried to clean their minds of any unwanted influences that might have tried to affect them.

"The easiest way I have found", he explained, "is to imagine myself on Jones' Peak on a breezy but warm summer's day. Close your eyes and picture yourself up there. You are looking out over the valley and the warm wind is blowing into your face, making your hair stream out behind you. As the wind blows over you, so it is taking away any nastiness in or around your body, mind and Soul… Feel it? It is both exhilarating and calming, but above all cleansing. What a wonderful feeling of purity, cleanliness and tranquillity".

The smell of Wild Gorse filled the room, then the clock on the mantelpiece gave a single 'ting'.

"That's it, my dear, it's eight o'clock already.

"Wow, Dad! That was fantastic… I could even smell the gorse on the mountains. The time went so quickly though. It didn't feel like an hour and a half to me".

"Tell me about it", he said with a twinkle in his eye, "I lost a week. I am glad that you could smell that gorse though, but it wasn't coming from the mountains. It was your mother's favourite perfume, and it is now her tell-tale… her calling card. Whenever you smell that, and it is unlikely to be from actual gorse, it will be your mother telling you that she is nearby".

"Thanks, Dad, this evening has been one of the best experiences in my life". She stood up, put her hands on his shoulder and kissed him on the forehead. "I'm really looking forward to our next session, but I have to be going now… I promised John…"

"Yes, I know… your John. My John is standing over there with your mother, another lady and Kiddy".

She looked, surprised, but could not see anyone.

"OK, bye, Dad; bye, Mum; bye, John and bye Kiddy until next week. Same time same place" she said and turned towards the front door. The 'other lady' waved and followed her out.

"That was vey successful, William" said John, while Sarah smiled proudly and clapped noiselessly.

∞

Four weeks after they had started on their sessions, they both wanted to meet like-minded people, so Becky took her laptop to her father's house one night, plugged her phone into the modem port and went on line. Searching on 'Spiritualism in Wales', she soon come across the NSU, which provided a list of Spiritualist Churches. They chose the closest and decided to go to their Sunday evening meeting, which started at six thirty.

It was located eight miles away, so Becky drove them there when the day came. Neither of them had set foot in a church since Becky got married and they had never been to a Spiritualist meeting. They were both a little nervous, but excited as well. Knowing that Sarah, John and Gwyneth, Becky's Guide, would be there was a big comfort.

One of the double front wooden doors was pinned open, so as they approached they could see the sparse congregation inside.

"Are you ready, Becky?"

"As ever I will be", she replied. "Let's go in".

They went through the door, William first. He span to his left when he heard Becky yelp behind him. A little old lady, whom neither of them had noticed sitting behind the door, had tapped her arm to offer her two hymn books.

"I'm sorry", she said, "I'm a little nervous".

"That's all right, dear. It was my fault. I didn't notice that you were new here. There aren't many of us, and everyone knows I sit here out of the draft. You don't know anyone here then?"

"No, we got your address from the Internet".

"Oh, I see. Well, you are most welcome. Gareth, do you have a minute, please, brother?" A tall handsome man in his fifties started to walk towards them, a welcoming smile on his face.

"We don't want to put anyone to any trouble", said William.

"It's no trouble. My name is Mary. Brother Gareth, this is ..."

"William and my daughter, Becky. We're from Bryn Teg, just up the road".

"My name is Gareth. Welcome to our small community William and Becky. I know Bryn Teg, I like to walk on the hilltop when I get the chance, which is a lot less often than I would like these days. Come in and sit down. We are just about to start. Have you been to a Spiritualist meeting before?"

"No, first one".

"No problem. I'll put you by Carwyn. He can show you the ropes. "Carwyn, this is William and his daughter, Becky. They are new to Spiritualism, can they sit by you?"

"Of course, Brother Gareth. Nice to meet you both".

There were about a dozen people when the service started with a hymn. After the hymn, Gareth welcomed everyone to the church, and gave a fifteen minute talk on the necessity of helping people in need, such as the Syrian refugees. He urged the congregation to increase their level of good Karma by acts of kindness towards strangers. Then they sang another hymn and Sister Emma talked for a few minutes then said that she had a few messages for people in the room.

"If Emma comes to either of you, stand up and speak to her. It doesn't have to be much. 'Good evening, Sister Emma' will do, but she wants to hear your voice. Just copy the others".

Emma went to three people, and then said, "I have a message for you, Brother".

"For me, Sister Emma?"

"No, for the Brother sitting next to you".

William stood up. "Good evening, Sister Emma".

"I have a lady here. She says, 'Surprise, surprise, Willy', does that mean anything to you, Brother?"

"Yes, Sister, my name is William".

"Good Brother William. She says that her name is Sarah and that she is your wife and your mother..." she said looking at Becky.

"That is correct, Sister Emma".

"Good. She says keep up the good work and that John, Gwyneth and Kiddy are here as well. Do you know those people?"

"The first two are people, but the third one only thinks that she is. She was, er, is our sheepdog". There was a round of hushed laughter from everyone there then Emma nodded at them. They sat down and she moved on to the next person for whom she had a message.

When Emma had finished, they sang a few more hymns and prayed for world peace and the service was over. Carwyn prevented them from rushing off, by commenting on their messages.

"That was very good for a first time" he said. "I have seen it before, but it is unusual. Messages start to come more regularly when your departed loved ones know where they can find you. Others get a strong urge to go to a specific church, because someone has a message for them, but yours didn't sound like one of those".

"No, it wasn't, Carwyn. I told my wife six days ago that we would be here tonight".

"Yes, that makes more sense. It is just that Gareth said you were complete beginners".

"Yes, we are, but we have read around the subject". Becky passed him a cup of tea with a biscuit on the saucer, and he gave it to Carwyn, before realising that everyone was getting one. Gareth brought Emma to them.

"Emma, I would like you to meet William and his daughter, Becky. William and Becky, this is Sister Emma, my wife.

"Nice to meet you", said Emma, "are you staying for the healing?"

They looked at each other.

"No, Emma, we didn't know anything about it, but we are not sick anyway", replied William.

"I have to be getting back too", said Becky.

"How about the Open Development Circle on Wednesday?" asked Gareth.

"Now that sounds most interesting, doesn't it, Becky? Can you make that?"

"It does sound interesting, but I would have to talk to my husband first".

"Of course, we understand, but you will be most welcome at both meetings. Here is my card, Becky", said Emma and Gareth gave one of his to William.

On their way home, they could talk only about the Spiritualist meeting they had just attended.

"I don't think that I'm interested in the healing. Are you, Becky? Is there anything the matter with you?"

"No, nothing the matter that a paracetamol doesn't cure, but I may find healing, giving healing, I mean, interesting one day. Time is my constraint, but I would like to be able to cure people. Wouldn't you?"

"Yes, I suppose so. I hadn't thought of it like that. I only thought that they wanted to heal me. Maybe one day, but the Development Circle? Yes, I want some of that".

A Night in Annwn

9. NEW HOBBIES

When Sally, the counsellor, came to the cottage on Monday morning for their fortnightly meeting, William had a lot to tell her. He sat her in Sarah's armchair and related the events that had occurred when he was in Annwn, as Sarah had told him. Sally recorded the interview and made notes as usual.

"And this further information came to you in a dream, did it, William?"

"No, I told you, Sarah was here and told me herself, when I said that my recollection was hazy".

"I see, you are one hundred percent certain that you were not asleep or dozing?"

"Yes, Sally", he replied starting to feel irritated. "I was sitting here and she was sitting there where you are... just like we are now".

"Here, in this very armchair?" she asked squirming a little and then feeling foolish for doing so.

"Yes", he answered smiling, his good humour returning, "and you're not sitting on her lap".

Sally smiled awkwardly. "That's a relief".

"I have something else to tell you too, Sally. Yesterday, Becky and me went to a Spiritualist Church meeting. We wanted to meet people who thought like we do. It was very interesting. The preacher's wife had a message for us from Sarah and our Spirit Guides, John and Gwyneth. She didn't say much, just 'Hello' basically, but she used my wife's secret nickname for me. Becky had heard it before, but knew that it was never used outside the house. It was the first time that Becky has had proof positive that Sarah is still alive".

"How did she react?"

"She already had a suspicion that there was life after death, because of the dream she had that I was in trouble, but this was the first time that she had it proved to her, so to speak. She couldn't talk about nothing else all the way back. She was very excited about it".

"Perhaps Becky could sit in on one of our meetings one day, it would be good to get her perspective on all this. I have some news for you too, William. I have been talking about your case with my colleagues and some of my former lecturers at university, and you are generating a great deal of interest. Yours is certainly the most clearly defined example of a near-death experience that I have ever come across... and that was before all the extra information you have given me today.

"So far, I have kept your name out of my case study, but I would like your permission to be able to publish your name in my report. What do you think?"

"I don't see why not... They are not going to want to interview me on News At Ten, are they? I'm not going to get hordes of them paparazzi camping on my lawn?"

"It is very unlikely, William", she said smiling at his intended exaggeration. "I'll be surprised if more than twenty people ever read my dissertation, but it is ethical to get your permission first".

"You carry on, Sally, and I'll ask Becky to sit in when you want her to".

"Thanks, William. I'd better let you get on with the rest of your day. Bye for now".

He showed her to the front door and waved her off. He hadn't told her about the Development Circles on purpose. Not yet. That would keep for another day.

∞

Becky had taken to phoning him when she started her ascent of their hill, so that William could start to brew the tea. She aimed at arriving just before six fifteen so that she could 'relax into the mood'.

William told her about Sally's visit, and she agreed to be interviewed if the timing was right. They had got into the habit of reading the next chapter out loud and discussing it. Then they would touch hands across the table, relax their minds, meditate on the lesson for a while and then try to put it into practice. They needed alarms to do this successfully, because otherwise the sections overran.

The method that worked for them, was to set Becky's phone to ping at seven, William's thirty minutes later and the mantelpiece clock at eight. It gave them three periods to use as they saw fit, because as Becky became more experienced, she had more say in what they learned and how. It had been Becky's idea to close each session with fifteen minutes of relaxation lying on the floor and William had taught her a method of calming the body that he had devised himself. It was very simple, but very effective, and he was working on a way of adapting it to the mental processes.

When they were finished, they sat in the armchairs. "I'm looking forward to the Development Circle in the church, Dad. It will be interesting to see how other people do it. Have you phoned Gareth to say that we are coming?"

"No, he said to just turn up".

"Yes, but it seems more polite to me to tell them that we will be there. I'll phone Emma tomorrow... pretend to be checking on the exact time... that sort of thing".

"I don't think you ought to be doing any pretending, just tell her we would like to go or ask her to confirm what time it starts. It strikes me that complete honesty is always the best policy in these matters. And I'm not being all high and mighty neither! I would lie to the government like they lie to us - without any trace of compunction, but it is not the same when you are dealing with intelligent, religious people".

"Yes, you are right, Da. I will phone her tomorrow".

When Becky had left, William put on his tracksuit bottoms and did his yoga exercises in the living room for thirty minutes, then he made himself a cheese sandwich and went to bed. He wanted to try out an idea he had had while meditating with Becky that evening.

He showered in the new bath that Becky and John had had installed in the box room when they converted it into an inside bathroom for him while he was in hospital. It was the first time that he had lived with one and he secretly found it very posh and rather decadent. He lit the large scented candle that stood on the bedside table in his otherwise Spartan room, put the electric light out and got into bed.

He started by silently repeating The Lord's Prayer. It was the only prayer he knew, but he had meditated on the words and found that he agreed with them wholeheartedly. Then he began his relaxation technique.

He imagined that all the major muscles in every major part of his body were controlled by miniscule men and women in factory overalls using hand-driven winches. He was their foreman, since it was his body. Starting in his left foot, he imagined himself walking from toe to toe inside his foot, giving each worker the night off. He ordered them to walk up his leg to his head and wait for him there.

He himself brought up the rear to ensure that all the workers received the message, then he did the same in the right leg. Once in the torso, he again gave everyone the night off, put his heart on autopilot, and cleared his arms in the same fashion. Likewise his shoulders and neck.

When he entered the Great Hall of his mind, all the workers were standing in groups chatting. He called for order and told them to jump out of his ears, but to return before daybreak. Most people took the paid holiday gratefully, but there were a few left when the others were gone.

Most of them were from the Ideas Brigade and they were a notoriously tough bunch to organise. This was where William's latest innovation came in

He ordered his mind to produce a crack in the floor and told the ideas and the others that they were going to play a game of Dare. The dare was to jump over the gap to prove their strength. Every time the macho men and women jumped over, some would not make it and disappear down the hole. William widened the crack each time until he stood alone in his body.

His innovation had worked, but the instant that he began to feel proud of himself, another idea appeared in the Hall. Soon, there were two others, as he tried to find a way to stop thinking. Obviously his idea needed tweaking, but he knew that he was onto something.

He awoke at the time that he had always considered normal when he was a working shepherd, at five o'clock, but he felt marvellous. It was one of the best night's sleep he had ever had, and certainly the best since Sarah had passed on. With the thought of her name, came the memory of a dream.

He had dreamed that he was in Annwn, but he assumed that he spent most of his dream time there these days. He had been sitting on a rock by a brook with Becky. Sarah, John and Gwyneth were also present, but they were seated on the other side of the water, although that was only a yard away. They had laughed and joked, and discussed the Development Circle that they would attend on Wednesday. It was frustrating, because William again felt that what he could remember was not all that had happened, and certainly not enough to fill the seven or eight hours that he had been asleep.

He got up nevertheless, went through his exercise regimen, showered, and went down to prepare his breakfast. He was learning how to cook as well. He had a couple of favourite daytime cookery programmes and would often write down the technique and ingredients of anything that took his fancy, so that he could get them when Becky took him shopping with her family on Saturday mornings.

Before his near-passing, as he referred to it, he had never tried to cook more than a fried breakfast, which he would eat at any time of the day if he was hungry and capable of cooking. Nowadays, though, he could cook Spaghetti Bolognese, Shepherd's Pie and several other dishes besides. His goal was to be able to prepare his own Sunday Roast.

He was aware that he was insanely backward in the culinary arts for a man of his age, but the way he saw it, progress was progress, and ultimately, that was all there was to it.

He had always been partial to lava bread, but he had previously always fried it with bacon. Becky had recently suggested frying it in a little butter and spreading it on dry toast like pate. That, and a mug of tea was going to be his breakfast for today.

Not only was it easier to prepare, but much healthier as well.

When he had eaten his breakfast and washed up, he set about the next major change in his lifestyle. He had never had a garden. Never, not even as a boy, and now that he didn't have a dog to take for a walk, he thought that he ought to have a hobby. Another daytime TV programme had given him the idea to start a garden.

Sarah had had a few flowers and bushes, but she had really only had time to tend her vegetable and herb patches. William thought that he could revive the overgrown herb garden, and plant some decorative flowers and plants as well. He liked flowers, he always had done, but had never had the time, until now.

He felt that he was becoming a normal human being for the first time in his life... he had been lopsided before.

He started by inspecting the front garden. He had walked through it at least four times every day throughout his life, unless he had been ill, but he had never really looked at it. The 'garden area' was not large, and at the moment, it was an overgrown mess, although Becky often took the shears to it. Despite the fact that not many people visited their hilltop, all those who did, had to pass his cottage at least twice, and suddenly he felt ashamed. He wanted passers-by to say, 'Oh, what a lovely cottage!' not 'Look at that derelict!'. He realized that he owed that to the community, the visitors, to Sarah and Becky, and to himself. Sarah's gardening tools were still hanging in the shed around the back, so he took a scythe, a rake and a wheelbarrow and started to hack the growth to the ground. He was going to begin over again, but if anything came up of Sarah's it could stay.

As he worked on the garden, he realized that he had been wallowing in self-pity for years, been letting everyone down and making a fool of himself. He apologised to Sarah, to the cottage and to their hill.

By midday, he had a pyramid of brambles, bracken and other unwanted species six feet high and six feet wide, then he went in for lunch.

He was ravenous and treated himself to a large can of draught Guinness and a makeshift Ploughman's Lunch. As he sat at the table in the front window to enjoy it and look at his handiwork, he had a feeling of déjà vu. A Ploughman's and a pint? He hadn't had that for years... but he had somewhere... but not Guinness... ale rang a bell. A Ploughman's and a pint of ale. He realized that it must have been in the pub in Annwn. Sarah had said that they had been in one within the castle, but she had not said what they had had. Now he was sure that he knew. He would have to ask her the next time he saw her.

When he had finished lunch he took his tools around to the back garden and surveyed the landscape with a slightly more experienced eye.

It was depressing.

The back garden was an area about five times the size of the front, and it was not so overgrown, because only a fifth of it had ever been cultivated - for the herbs and vegetables - but that bit was a total mess as well. He began to see himself as others had probably been seeing him since Sarah had passed on – a derelict of his former self. Not much more than a shabby tramp except that he had a house to live in – a house that he had neglected as much as Sarah's gardens.

He felt ashamed of himself, and so started to work with enthusiasm and masochism. It crossed his mind that he might overexert himself and have another heart attack – perhaps a fatal one this time, but that did not deter him. He welcomed the idea, but did not really expect so much luck. Then Sarah's words in Annwn sounded in his head.

'Please, Willy, don't talk like that... You chose to be born in a certain place and with certain people because that environment was the best you could find to teach you the lessons you wanted to learn. It is a long and hard road to get where you are today, do not even consider giving up before your journey is at an end. Nothing is worth that. Be patient, have courage and see your life out'.

"All right, my darling Sarah, I will never wish for an end to my life on the Surface again. I will do that for you, and I will restore our home and your gardens to the best of my ability in your memory. You loved it here, and showed your love by the way you looked after the place and I am going to learn by your example.

"God, it has taken me long enough, hasn't it?"

As he cleared away the brambles and bracken, a vestige of Sarah's garden could still be seen. It was pitiful, but it was enough to bring back memories of how it had looked in its heyday.

"I won't let you down again, my girl… never again. You'll see if I don't…"

He clipped at the invading wild plants more carefully with secateurs so as not to disturb the plants beneath that his wife had planted with her own hands, then dragged them away to add to his heap.

She had marked out the perimeter of the patch with unusual rocks that they had found on the hill, and delineated the internal boundaries assigned to individual species of herbs with pebbles that their friends and family had brought back for her by the bucket load when they had been to the coast.

Most of it was still in place, though a little dilapidated where they had been pushed aside by the wild flowers. He went for the trowel and hand fork that he had seen hanging in the shed, got down on his knees and started to turn the top soil over as he had seen Sarah and other gardeners do in the past.

When he had finished his first pass over the patch, for he was thinking about the double-digging that he remembered his father talking about, he tried to get up, but had to use the fence to pull himself up. His back and his knees were sore. He also made a mental note that the fence needed another coat of paint. Leaning on the fence, and arching his back with a hand in the small, he surveyed the perimeter fence.

'That's another job that needed doing years ago'. The wind on the hill threw dust at paint and stain like a constant sand-blaster, but he hadn't painted it for at least five or six years. When he felt a little better, he stepped back to survey his handiwork.

The plot was bare. There was at most twenty-five percent of the coverage that had used to be there, and it was in poor condition – yellow, straggly and sickly-looking from the lack of light. He faintly heard the chimes of the mantelpiece clock and looked at his watch. It was five o'clock. He could hardly believe that he had spent four hours on that patch, although he was proud of it.

'I'll dig it over again tomorrow', he thought and started for the house, when he suddenly turned around and went back to the plot and picked up his tools. 'Start as you mean to go on' he told himself and hung the tools on their hooks in the shed before going in.

He washed his hands and face at the kitchen sink and admired his plot again. He just had to tell Becky what he had been doing all day. So, he collected his new phone from the table in the living room and went back out to call her where the signal was usually better. It occurred to him to take a photo and send that first. Becky had shown him how to do it when they had bought the mobile a fortnight before, but this would be the first time he had done it on his own.

He took the photo, clicked on Becky's name when it asked for the recipient, sent it and phoned her.

"What do you think of your old Da now then, my dear? I'm turning out to be a bit of a whizz kid, aren't I?"

"Yes, we'll have you using the Internet on a laptop computer next. Oh, Dad, I'm so proud of the way you have sharpened yourself up lately. We were becoming so worried about you. Anyway, that herb garden is looking good. We'll have to call into the garden centre on Saturday and stock up on some more plants, won't we?"

"Yes, but not only herbs. I did the front garden too this morning, but I might have been a bit heavy-handed there – it's completely barren. I gave it a thorough scalping and all this gardening has shown me what a poor condition the fence is in, so I need a gallon of fence paint and a new four-inch brush as well".

"Wow! The next time I come to the house I won't recognise it – I'll probably drive right past it. You didn't overdo it, you don't think, Dad?"

"No, I'm as fit as a fiddle after all that yoga", he fibbed.

"Are you sure? Gardening is notoriously strenuous on the back and you have never done any before, so if you are not hurting right now after a day in the garden, you sure as eggs will be tomorrow… and we're going to the Circle, don't forget".

"No, I haven't forgotten. I'm looking forward to it".

"I reckon you will be lucky if you can get there. You need to soak in a hot bath, that's what you need".

"Yes, good idea. I still got an old box of them crystals your mother used to use somewhere, I'll use those…"

"We threw all that old stuff out when we renovated the place! That box was empty! The crystals had either been used or evaporated years ago. You can't keep them in an open box for ever, you know!"

"Can't you? Oh, I didn't know…"

"Just have a hot bath and use plenty of soap. It will help anyway, and we'll get some more smellies on Saturday. Oh, I have to go now, the boys are back from school. I'm proud of you, Dad, I'll see you tomorrow evening. Bye".

"Bye, love".

He felt a strange twinge of regret that she had thrown out Sarah's toiletries, even if they were no good any longer.

He arched his back again and had an idea. He looked in the pantry, found what he wanted, made himself a couple of cheese and ham sandwiches, and took two tins of Guinness out of the fridge.

'I'm not up to yoga tonight', he thought, 'anyway I've had plenty of exercise'.

Then he took his collection of items upstairs and began to run his bath. After adjusting the taps to provide a flow of water that was not too hot, he tipped salt from the large plastic container onto the palm of his hand and sprinkled it onto the water, and then did it again for good measure. Then he dropped two teabags into the water, took the small container of dried rosemary that he had been keeping for the first time he cooked roast lamb, and emptied that into the water, and finally gave three long squirts of washing-up liquid.

'That will do nicely', he said to himself, pulling up a chair to act as a bath side table. Then he opened a can, switched his old transistor radio on, and got into the bath.

"Ah, luxury!" he said out loud as he reached for a tin of Guinness and a sandwich.

10. THE DEVELOPMENT CIRCLE

When William awoke the next morning, his back hurt although it had not prevented him from getting a good night's sleep. He lay in bed hoping that it would have been worse if he hadn't had his own-style herbal bath, but he had no way of knowing. After a visit to the bathroom, he hobbled back to his bedroom and attempted to do his yoga exercises, but he had to skip most of them. He wondered whether a hair of the dog, in the form of more gardening might help. He decided to give it a try after breakfast, so he got dressed and went downstairs.

He reached into a kitchen cupboard for his backache pills. He hadn't had to take any since he had been in hospital, but he needed them again now. He took two, the maximum dose in four hours, with a glass of water, and put the kettle on. He fancied a bowl of porridge, but he had never made it before. He was undaunted though, because while shopping the weekend before, Becky had assured him that the recipe on the packet was easy to follow. He took a cup of tea through to the living room and read the instructions twice.

He was confident that he could manage it. Twenty minutes later he was back at his table with his porridge and another cup of tea, feeling quite proud of himself. He noticed that the tablets had dulled the pain as well, so, he put three large potatoes in a low oven, pulled on his walking boots, took the tools from the shed and inspected the herb patch.

He was certain that the plants looked both greener and stronger than they had seventeen hours before when he had last seen them. It was ample reward for the effort he had put in, and even compensated for having had back pain.

"What do you think of that then, Sarah?" he asked under his breath.

He was half-hoping for a reply, but didn't receive one, so put a small square of mat that he had noticed in the shed, on the grass, knelt on it and started to turn the soil over. It was easier this time and the mat saved his knees a little.

As he worked, speckles of green floated down past his eyes. 'I've heard of green fingers,' he said to himself, 'but never no green dandruff'. It puzzled him as he continued, until he realized that it must be rosemary from his bath the night before. 'Well, I'll be!' he exclaimed, laughing out loud and he shook his head to produce a flurry of the green herb.

Two hours later, he was preparing his lunch of two baked potatoes stuffed with cottage cheese and a little diced ham together with a bag of fresh salad for one and another cup of tea. He would have the third one before he went to church, and maybe they could stop in a chip shop on the way back for a rare treat.

After lunch, he turned his attention to the front garden and worked at turning the soil over there with a full size garden fork, but he only worked for two hours as he didn't want to overdo it. Then he ran himself another bath, omitting the green herbs, and meditated in the bath until five. Becky was due at six and he had another potato to eat.

Becky was punctual, as she usually was, and they had a little time, so she wanted to see the gardens before they left.

"I'm impressed", she said "and I bet Mum is too. Let me take a few photos quickly. Stand over there by your garden, Percy Thrower".

"Yes, all right, less of the lip!" he joked.

They arrived at the Bethesda Spiritualist Church ten minutes early and went in. Mary was not behind the door because there was no service as such. Gareth called them to enter further when he saw them standing just inside the doorway. The rows of chairs from Sunday had been folded away and twelve of them were arranged in a circle in the middle of the floor.

"Come in, come in! I am so glad that you could make it. How are you both keeping?"

They exchanged pleasantries and then Gareth showed them to their chairs in the Circle.

"Excuse me a moment". He scooted off and returned minutes later with Mary and Carwyn whom he placed either side of them. "We will be starting very soon", explained Gareth. "If you want to use the toilets first, they are through that door at the end".

Gareth stood at the stage end on the Circle, a seat away from Mary and held up a hand. Thank you Brothers and Sisters, I would like you to show a warm welcome to two new members of our Circle this evening, William and Becky". There followed nodding and smiles from everyone present. "Thank you", he continued. "Now I will hand over to Sister Mary to lead this evening's meeting. Sister Mary... Brother David, the lights, please". Whereupon the lights were lowered just enough to remove any harshness, although it was still broad daylight outside, since it didn't get dark in June until about ten o'clock.

"Good evening, Brothers and Sisters. I am happy to see you all here tonight. Would you please assist me to open this Development Circle in the time-honoured way. Please take the hand of those sitting next to you and join me in reciting the Lord's Prayer". When they were done, they released each other's hands and Mary spoke again. "For the benefit of our latest members, if you prefer to carry out any part of the meeting with your eyes closed, please feel free to do so". William looked around and saw that most people did have their eyes closed.

"We are going to continue by cleansing our minds of our Earthly strife. I want to tell you how I do that, but if you have your own favourite method, please use it. Where I refer to myself, you should imagine yourself.

"I picture myself on a diving board, sometimes naked, sometimes not. This time not, since I have told you about it". There was a ripple of subdued laughter. "The huge pool beneath me is empty and a warm breeze is blowing in my face. I am completely at ease, then I dive into the water with the grace of an Olympic athlete. The water is wonderful. I can feel it taking away all my problems, aches and pains as I go down and then begin to rise to the surface. I have all the air and time that I need and I know that when I get to the Surface, I will be in total harmony with the Universe.

"I will give you a few minutes to experience that, before we continue. Good, you are now at ease and clean in mind and body.

"I swim to the far side of the pool and walk up the steps into the sunshine and before me is a field of very tall wheat. The smell is fantastic, so it draws me in, although the stalks are over my head.

"Try that, please.

"As you walk through the lush wheat, who do you meet, or what do you come across? I will leave you to discover for yourself for thirty minutes. Have fun".

When the time had elapsed, Mary called everyone back to the church, and gave them time to come around. William could plainly see that some people needed more time than others.

"All right, Brothers and Sisters, I hope that you all came across something or someone. Starting with Brother Gareth and moving to his left, I would like you all to share your walk through the wheat field with us. Please don't feel that you have to tell us everything, if some of it is private. Brother Gareth..."

All twelve of them told of their experience and when they were finished, Mary asked Emma for her comments.

"I would like to say that the woman I saw on Sunday with William and Becky, Sarah, is here again. She is laughing and says that green dandruff suits you William. I have no idea what that means, but I hope that it means something to you. I would also like to say that I see a silver trumpet hanging from your earlobe. Excuse me, it is not effeminate, it is more in the style of a sailor..." Gareth coughed.

"Oh, dear", said Emma", it looks as if time has beaten us again. I will hand you back to Sister Mary".

"Thank you, Sister Emma. Brothers and Sisters, please help me to close the Circle by singing 'Abide With Me' and then taking a moment to return your thoughts to your worldly affairs. Abide with me..."

David, the lights, please" said Gareth a minute after they had stopped singing.

Gareth and Emma broke the Circle by removing their chairs and placing a table in the centre of everyone. David put a tray of cups and saucers on it and went for the tea and cake while Gareth stood the cups the right way up. Emma was looking at everyone in turn.

"Has everyone come back?" she asked solicitously. People nodded at her and smiled. Most of the sitters wanted to remain behind and discuss their experiences in more detail, but others wanted to leave after their tea. William and Becky left as soon as it seemed polite to be able to.

"Thank you for inviting us, Gareth and Emma, we have had a truly eye-opening experience. Mary's technique was very easy and produced good results, didn't it, judging by what everyone said that they saw in the wheat field after their swim".

"In fact, it was her first time leading a meeting on her own, but she did do very well", replied Gareth walking them to the door

"We have to go back now, but I hope that you will tell her that we enjoyed the experience tremendously. Becky has to get home, you see".

"Yes, well, busy lives, eh? I hope that you will be able to make it on Sunday. Goodbye for now. I'm not sure where Emma is..."

"Say 'Goodbye' for us, Gareth. Bye".

As they were driving back, William suggested fish and chips from their village and Becky agreed. "Do you have time to bring them back to the cottage to eat them?"

"No, I'm afraid not, not tonight, Da, but I will next week, now that we know the routine".

"All right, love, I understand. Who'd have thought it, eh? Game old bird, isn't she?"

"Who, Da?"

"That Mary. She's got to be a hundred, but she still likes to think of herself swimming naked in the open air and then running though the wheat fields in the all-together looking for people to talk to".

"Dad! You do come out with them, don't you? The whole point of this evening's meeting was to concentrate on the inner being and ignore the outer shell, and you have to think of that!"

"Actually, I have been trying not to think of her standing on a diving board naked since she put the image in my mind. Perhaps a chicken and mushroom pie, chips and mushy peas will help. I don't think I could face a crinkly battered cod right now".

"You are awful".

"Listen to me, my girl. I didn't have my eyes closed this evening, and when she said that, all the men looked as if they had been sucking on a particularly bitter lemon. It might not be politically correct, but you are fooling yourself if you don't think that that is what men think. I'm not saying that anyone has the right to say it to her, because they don't, but I have the right to think it and say it to my daughter in private".

"All right, let's get you your pie and get you home before it goes cold.

That night in bed after his pie and chips and limited yoga exercises because of his meal, he went into his relaxation and meditation routine. The question on his mind was what can a silver trumpet earring pendant mean?

In the pitch-black of the Great Hall of his mind, a faint glow appeared in what could be described as the centre of one of the narrower walls. It was just enough light for him to make out a stage and rows of seats like in a cinema. The first row was just behind him, so he sat down.

As he was making himself comfortable John appeared on the stage. "Good evening, William", he said.

"Good evening, John. Thank you for being near so often".

"That is my pleasure. I am here tonight to answer a question that has been building up in your mind for some time now and of which you had another example tonight. Namely, symbolism.

"We all, every sentient creature, who has lived or is living on the Surface of this world or any other, has developed speech of some kind in order to communicate with our fellows, and the colour, or variety of that language was influenced by the lifestyle of the speaker. In other words the metaphors, similes and symbolism that everybody uses in their everyday speech are affected by their daily activities.

"Am I making myself clear, William?"

"Yes, John, thank you".

"Good. Nations can have a tendency to use one set of symbols, but within that nation, there can be other sub-groups as well. Britain is a seafaring nation and so, naturally, references to the sea are common, but there were always farmers and weavers, the young and the old, male and female, et cetera. Once you are aware of this, you will notice it early on in any conversation.

"With that in mind, I would like to show you something, an, er, film. Yes, a film". John stepped back into the darkness and a projection canvas of about nine by six feet appeared. A film began to roll.

It was an external shot of a small galleon with three masts. What William imagined as Eighteenth Century Jack Tars were manning the vessel as it sailed out of a calm bay towards the open sea. The sailors looked happy enough and were singing as they went about their tasks. The film froze and John stepped into the light reflected by the screen.

"If you dreamed that", he said tapping the screen with a baton that materialised in his hand, "what would you think it meant?"

"Er, I'm not sure, John… Perhaps, I had been watching an historical drama recently?"

"All right, that is possible. Do you remember the difference between meaningful dreams and mental filing?" William nodded, "So, if this dream disappears quickly you would probably be right, but what if it stayed with you all day? What then?"

"Er, I might be on the edge of starting an adventure?"

"Exactly! Now you are getting the hang of it. I was a sailor and a fisherman, so if I am going to try to tell you something, I am far more likely to use this kind of symbolism than an aeroplane pilot might or a seamstress". He tapped the screen again, disappeared and the film continued.

As the galleon left the bay, a lookout in the rigging screamed, "Spanish warship off the port bow!" The men on deck jumped to action while the officers barked orders at their men to prepare to flee because they were unarmed. "Skull and Crossbones", shouted the lookout.

"Damn", muttered the captain with a telescope to one eye. "A Jolly Roger. Hard to starboard! All hands on deck! Mr Richards…" His orders were repeated by his First Mate. The film stopped again.

"And now, William?"

"I suppose, it could mean to be on guard because even though things seem to be going well, there is trouble around the corner".

"Could do… this is only an example, of course. A real dream would probably be more specific. Anyway…" He stepped back and it started again.

As every working man was busy with unfurling more sail, they heard a boom, and William saw a puff of smoke cloud a portion of the pirate raider. It was a lucky shot and the thirty-two-pounder crashed into the main mast throwing eight men into the sea. The mast toppled slowly to the deck like a felled tree. It did not crush anyone, but several men were fouled in the rigging. Deckhands rushed for the axes, which were hanging around the ship in order to cut their friends free.

"That is a good example", said John stepping into the light again as the film stopped. "If you saw a man coming at you with an axe in a dream, you would probably be frightened, but having seen this film and knowing my background, you now realise that an axe is one of the most useful tools a sailor had… that and his knife". The light was turned up a little and the screen disappeared.

"Do you see the point, William? You are not in a position to interpret even your own dreams, until you know what the symbols mean… Why, it is like trying to interpret a language that you have only heard once. The same goes for trying to decipher other people's dreams. It is almost impossible from their retelling of the dream alone, because the narrator will miss out and misinterpret details. It is inevitable.

"This means that you cannot learn how to do this during one watch, er, overnight. It takes a long time to build up a vocabulary of symbols so that we can communicate quickly in that fashion – when it would be impossible to talk. At the moment we can only talk when you are in this condition, which means for a short period once a day.

"However, if we had a set of symbols, we could communicate all day".

"Yes, I can see that. So, I have been wondering why Emma told me she could see a trumpet dangling from my ear…"

"Yes, but that was me trying to tell her something and it illustrates what I have just been telling you very clearly. Who wore earrings?"

"Ladies, gypsies, er… Oh! Sailors!"

"Exactly! So if she had known anything about me, which she cannot be expected to, a symbol pendant on an earring might suggest that I am trying to say something. And the trumpet?"

"No, idea. I have never held one, and can't play one, nor any other kind of musical instrument for that matter…"

"No, but there are other forms of trumpet… think".

"A speaking trumpet? Or a hearing trumpet… an old fashioned hearing trumpet!"

"Yes, I used to use one on the Surface, but thousands of people did. Especially ex-gunners, artillerymen. You could go deaf during one battle. Imagine being on a gun deck on a man o' war in a sea fight! It was horrendous… Old John Hawkins' frigates could have a hundred and twenty-four guns on three decks! Fifty-six cannon firing a broadside every few minutes in a confined space. My word, you needed a hearing aid after that".

"Anyway, I was trying to give Emma a message to give to you, but you didn't give her time to think about it. When someone gives you a message, it is only fair really to give them enough time to think and to explain. I am certain that she would have got my meaning.

"I was trying to tell her that you have the potential to hear Spirit very well and that you are a good listener by nature whether it be to Spirit or your fellow human beings on the Surface".

"I see. Easy when you know how, isn't it?"

"Isn't almost everything? You see, William, all we are trying to do, you and I, is learn how to communicate with one another. This is nothing new. Families the Universe over and throughout time have done this with babies and so have people and their Guides. Everyone gets there in the end, it is just that some take longer than others, but that is not important. The trick, if there is one, is to keep trying – never to give up.

"You are taking all the right steps, and your progress is impressive. Part of your success is due to your enthusiasm and part because you are going over old ground. You are relearning what you knew before you came here. It is common for people to forget, and then be shocked back into taking an interest in Spiritual affairs by an event. Your Self has known the benefits of taking such an interest, so it will not allow its Earthly representative, that is you, to lose that interest for long.

"It is the reality of what you heard before that once Spirit has you, it will never let you go. It is you, not Spirit, that will never allow you to give up… or your Spirit Self at any rate".

"My Soul?"

"That is as good a word as any. You realise deep down how progress in life is really measured. Your Self, Spirit Self or Soul is always fully aware of it, and it, that is you, will nag yourself until you get back on track. Of course, this can take a long time, when measured in Earth years.

"I will leave you to rest now, William. Just keep doing what you are doing and you will get there soon enough. Good night".

"Good night, John", he thought, "and thanks…"

11. SPIRITUAL HEALING

On Thursday and Friday, William worked in his gardens front and back for most of the day and took a hot bath every evening. His back still hurt, but he had known worse and he was giving it a lot of punishment. However, the previous yoga exercises, the painkillers and the hot baths were keeping the discomfort to a tolerable level. When Saturday morning came, his gardens were ready to be planted and he knew which plants, flowers and herbs he wanted. He had made a list and a schematic diagram to help him remember where to put them.

Becky and John arrived at ten to do the main weekly shop for the two households.

"OK, Da, have you got everything on your shopping list?"

"Yes, thanks, everything has been ticked off. I'm going to try my first Sunday Roast tomorrow, then Shepherd's Pie with the leftovers on Monday. That will last me two days, then there's... yes, I've got plenty. I may need another loaf on Wednesday, but let's not worry about that now".

"OK, as long as you are sure. Do you still want to go to the garden centre?"

"Oh yes! That is the highlight of this weekend's shopping. I don't know what to be more excited about: cooking my first Sunday Roast or planting my first flowers. Heady days, my dear girl!"

"As long as you're happy, Da, that's the main thing. OK, John, the garden centre it is next, please, love".

"Your wish is my command, but don't forget all the food in the boot. I don't think we ought to stay there more than thirty minutes".

"Yes, all right, Mr. Sensible. Dad doesn't want much, do you, Dad?"

"I have a list. Perhaps we could give it to a sales person and they could find everything more quickly than we could?"

"Good idea, Da".

The garden centre had about four-fifths of what William wanted and offered to order the shortfall for him by the following Saturday, which he accepted after checking with his son-in-law that that would be all right.

He was excited as he and the others carried his bags into the kitchen for him to sort out in his own time, since they were worried about the condition of their own perishable food on that warm afternoon in late June. William didn't mind their rushing off. He felt like a child on Christmas Morning. First he put his food away, and then he took his plants outside and stood them in the shade of the cottage. Next he washed his hands, made himself two double cheese and ham sandwiches, took a Guinness from the fridge and went into the lounge to brush up on the plants that he had bought in the general purpose gardening book he had treated himself to in the supermarket. All of the plants that he already had and those he was waiting for were in it.

At six o'clock, he went into the garden, transferred the fittings from Sarah's old perished garden hose to his new one, fitted his new spray gun attachment to the front and had a bit of fun watering the garden in preparation for planting the next day.

He wanted everything to be just right, in order to give himself the highest chance of success. It would be Sarah's birthday on July 15th and he wanted her gardens to look in good shape by then, even though he was unsure whether the Earth birthday of someone who had already passed over meant anything to them anymore.

That night, he peeled the potatoes, carrots and parsnips and cut them to size in front of the television as he had seen Sarah do for decades, realizing for the first time that she had not been doing it because she was bored, but because she wanted to steal a march on the next day, which was what he wanted to do too.

Bored with the television by nine o'clock, he took a bath, did his exercises, or most of them, and went to bed to meditate and sleep.

Sunday was going to be a big day.

His first job in the morning, after a shower and yoga, was to place his leg of lamb, the parsnips and some of the potatoes in the baking tray, brush them with olive oil and besprinkle them with herbs. Then he put them in the oven, lit the gas and set the alarm clock. When that went off, he would have to light the gas under the potatoes and another ten minutes later, drain fat from the tray and start to make the gravy. He had two hours and forty minutes in the garden first though, so he set the new music centre, which Becky and John had given him for his birthday, to Radio Three, turned the volume up and opened the windows so he would be able to hear it outside.

He decided to work on the north-facing front garden first, because it was in the shade of the hill. He could work on the back garden later when the sun was not so hot, although he had to be ready for church by six. The classical music from the radio spurred him on.

His Sunday Roast was fabulous, even if he had to say so himself. The only snag was the gravy, and that was because he had insisted on making it like Sarah had, with corn flour, fat from the meat and water from the potatoes, against Becky's advice. He also knew where he had gone wrong - by adding the flour directly to the hot liquid, and not mixing it with cold water first. Still, he had learned his lesson, and he didn't mind his lumpy gravy anyway.

After lunch, he felt like a nap, so he put the television on, found a rugby game, opened a can of Guinness and dozed in front of the box. He awoke at three twenty, cleared the table and wished that he had done it before he started to watch the game, washed up and looked at the time. It was four fifteen, too late to start again outside, so he sat in front of the television again and finished his now warm can.

William was ready for Becky when she arrived. She had a quick look at the front garden, gave her seal of approval, and they left.

"My roast leg of lamb went well this afternoon", he said as they were driving along.

"I'm pleased for you, Da. How did the gravy turn out?"

"It was gorgeous, just like your mother used to make... except for the lumps..."

They both laughed.

"You could tip that into the Shepherd's Pie and turn it into a lamb and potato pie".

"I don't mind really. I know my mistake. It won't happen again, but I like your suggestion. Shall we stop for fish and chips on the way home? My treat".

"Yes, sure. Everyone in our house enjoyed that on Wednesday".

"Becky, all this gardening has brought my old back trouble back. Will you have time to stop for a bit of healing tonight?"

"Aw, I'm sorry, Da, if you had given me some notice, I could have arranged it with John, but it is awkward with his shifts... Is it really bad?"

"No, dear, it's not that bad. I didn't do so much this weekend. To tell you the truth, I am more curious as to how Gareth and his team go about giving healing. Don't you worry about it".

"Perhaps next week, Dad, if you still want to".

"Yes, sure. Don't you give it another thought, my girl".

The church service went as it had before, and Sarah and their Guides had messages of encouragement for them. When it was over, they sought Emma out.

"Sister Emma", said William. "I have been thinking about what you said on Wednesday about a silver trumpet hanging from my ear. What do you think that meant? I have never played a trumpet in my whole life".

"Oh, yes, I remember. Oh, I see! No. Oh, my gosh! I didn't mean that sort of trumpet. If it was a musical instrument, it was more like a post horn, but I saw it as a listening trumpet... one of those old fashioned hearing aids and it was silver to show that it was important".

"It isn't your fault, Sister Emma, we had to rush off. I didn't give you time to explain. I apologise. What significance did that listening trumpet have for you, Emma, because hanging from my ear, it could not have been meant for me".

"It was obviously meant for someone to see and report to you, in my opinion, but to me, a listening trumpet improves hearing, so anyone with a listening trumpet has improved, or enhanced hearing abilities. Since this is a class for psychic phenomena, I would guess that it means that you have the potential to hear Spirit, and perhaps better than most. It might also mean that you are a good listener in general and so might make a good counsellor.

"Does that make any sense to you?"

"Oh, yes. It ties up a lot of loose ends. Thank you very much, Sister".

After the service, William sought out Gareth during the tea break.

"Brother Gareth, I wonder if I may have a quick word with you before you start your healing".

"Certainly, Brother, how can I help you?"

"It is to do with healing. My daughter and I are both interested in healing, giving healing, but she has problems staying behind on Sunday night for one reason or another. So I was wondering whether you could recommend a book to us that we could read at home".

"Yes, there are several. Basically, you want to read about how the body is made up on a Spiritual level. Traditional Western medicine treats the physical body, but Spiritual healing works in a different way. We believe that physical illness is the external manifestation of a Spiritual or psychic imbalance. Therefore, our form of healing sets out to correct that imbalance.

"I often look at it as a jelly mould. If your jelly mould has a dent in it, every jelly that you make will have a defect. Traditional Western medicine tries to correct that defect by cutting it off or filling it in. However, we go back to the jelly mould and attempt to knock out the dent".

"That makes it very clear, Brother. I like that analogy".

"Thank you. We have a small reference library here in the church for members only, I will see if there is a relevant book in at the moment. One minute".

He returned with a book, but stopped off on the way to get the healing session started.

"You are in luck. This is very good, now I have to go. You may keep it until next Sunday, if you wish".

"Thank you", he said inspecting the cover. "Er, one last question, please? Can you heal yourself?"

"Certainly! 'Physician, heal thyself!' is one of our phrases. Everybody is constantly healing themselves. The problem comes when the sick person is too weak to be able to manage it, which is when they have to seek outside help, which is why I must rush off now. I'll see you later if you are still here. Enjoy the book".

As they were driving home from the chip shop, William flicked through the book. "Gareth recommended this one to me, The Light That Heals, by Colin Jones. You are interested in this aspect of Spiritualism too, aren't you, Becky?"

"Yes, very much so. John suffers from a bad back because of his work, and the kids are always getting aches and pains - growing pains really, headaches, stomach aches and other small things like that. I would love to be able to help more than just giving them a tablet".

"OK, well, I know that I will be reading this until I can't anymore tonight, so why don't we take a look at it together tomorrow night?"

"Yeah, sounds good to me".

"All right, love" he said as he got out of the car outside his cottage, "thanks for the lift. I'll see you tomorrow".

"Sarah, I'm home", he said closing the door behind him, but not yet putting the light on in case she was there. When she wasn't he flicked the switch and sat at the table with his book to eat his cod, chips and mushy peas.

Well over an hour later, William noticed that it was getting dark outside, so he reluctantly had to leave his book and water the unplanted herbs and the garden. While he was there an idea came to him for Kiddy's grave. He had been wondering how to mark it for sometime, and the solution presented itself in one. In fact, it was so clear that he asked himself whether it was an example of his newly discovered ability to listen. Perhaps someone in Annwn had suggested it. He chuckled at the thought, but hoped that it was true.

When he was done, William took his book into the bath with him, did his yoga exercises thereafter and then read until well past midnight. His theme for meditation that night was Spiritual Healing, but he fell asleep before he could get the workers to jump out of his ears and he dreamed that he had a picnic with Sarah and Kiddy under a Mountain Ash on their hill.

Despite his late night, William got up at seven, did his exercises and made his breakfast of a boiled egg with a runny yolk and soldiers of toast to dip in it. His dream seemed linked to his ideas of the previous evening about Kiddy's grave, so he changed his plans. He watered the herbs instead of planting them, and watered the rest of the garden too, then set off up the hill with his stave and a hessian sack containing a few tools over his shoulder like a swagman.

Less than halfway to the summit, he saw what he knew was there, but wanted to collect it on the way home, so he continued on up. He ignored the seat this time and looked for a grassy patch where he could sit and read his book. It was the ideal spot to study and it was his intention to remain there until noon. The heat of the morning sun was mitigated by the breeze, but William was no fool. He had spent all his life on this hill. His face was shaded under the wide brim of an ancient leather hat and the skin that was exposed was tough and leathery also. He felt that if he had questions about the content of the book, this would be the place to get the answers.

He had never read the like before, but it seemed to him that he must have because it all made so much sense to him.

At twelve o' clock, later than he had intended, he took a pack of cheese sandwiches and a bottle of tap water out of his sack and enjoyed lunch, then he looked around for some wild flowers for Kiddy's grave. There were no flowers as such, he knew that, but he was looking for clover. There were usually plenty of the white and pink varieties now that there were no sheep to graze on them. He dug up six of each colour and started down again.

He stopped at the two Mountain Ash trees that he had passed that morning. One was fully grown, but the other was a sapling from the previous year. He dug it up and put it in his sack with the clover.

When he got home, he planted the Mountain Ash a little south of the grave, but only two feet, so that it would provide some shade from the midday sun for his dog, and planted the clover in a circle of alternating colours around the spot where he could still see that John had dug out. William was pleased with the result, but there was still one thing missing, so he phoned his daughter, watered the plants and tree in and set off down the hill.

It was gone four o'clock before he found what he wanted, so he walked on down to the pub and phoned Becky on the way to pick him up there.

She walked into the pub at six o'clock and could not believe her eyes. Her father was sitting at the bar playing Crib with Dai with a slimline bitter lemon drink before him. Harry noticed her before William did and shrugged when she pointed at his drink.

"I don't know, love. I have never seen him do it before. Is he on medication or summat?"

"Dad! I have never seen you not drink beer in a pub!"

"No, but there's a first time for everything, and we've got something to do. All right, Dai. I'll give you that game. Here's your winnings. Come on, Becky, let's get started".

As they were driving up the hill, William announced, "Becky, remember that spot where you found us that time?"

"How could I ever forget?"

"I want you to stop there, please".

A quarter of a mile further on, Becky pulled over. They sat in the car for a few minutes, each with their own thoughts of that night.

"Come on, let's have a closer look. Where did you find us exactly?"

"By there, by that rock", she said pointing down.

"Yes, I thought so. I came up the hill behind Kiddy and saw her in trouble by there. She was gone by the time I could get to her, so I picked her up, but couldn't stand up with the extra weight – my knees, you know. I pulled us up onto our boulder and put Kiddy on my lap, but then had a heart attack myself and we both slid off again. I thought we must have landed by there.

"That is the rock I must have bashed my head on, but the other one I put there this afternoon. Give me a hand to get it into the car. Open the boot, darling, now give me a hand up. Yes, that's it".

He placed the five-kilo rock in the boot and they took it home.

"I have another surprise for you", he said lugging the rock around the back of the cottage".

"Oh, it's beautiful, Da!" she declared as he sank to his knees and started to dig a shallow hole between the clover and the tree. He placed the naturally mitred stone in its foundation and stood up.

"Yes, I think it is too, even if I say so myself. It came to me yesterday while I was in the garden, and then I dreamed about it too. After that there was nothing I could do but make it reality. I'm so glad you like it as well".

"Shall we say a little prayer, Dad?"

"Yes, all right. A silent prayer and then 'Abide with Me', I think".

When their little funeral service was over, Becky took her father's hand as they walked inside.

"That was lovely, Dad. I could never have imagined you doing anything like that a couple of months ago".

"No, perhaps not… Let's read that book. I started it last night, and I was reading it on our peak this morning. I find it fascinating and want you to hear about it too".

They took it in turns to read a couple of pages, but they had little time to get through more than the introduction.

"We are going to have to leave it there for tonight, but I will run through the most important points for you and fill in a few gaps before we close.

"Basically you are channelling energy into the sick person, so that they have enough strength to heal themselves. You can think of it as recharging their battery, which has run down too far because of overuse due to sickness or neglect. You channel that energy through your hands into the other person's body, usually at the point where the sickness manifests itself.

"By the way, as an aside. Have you noticed how everybody holds or touches the part of them that hurts? You can always tell someone with a bad back because their hand will be on it. Even Hollywood knows it, because when someone gets shot, their hand goes straight to the entry wound! They are not trying to staunch the flow of blood, they are trying to reduce the pain".

His hand shot out and rapped the knuckles of his daughter's left hand.

"Ow!" she said, putting her right hand over them. "That hurt! What did you do that for? We're not in school now, you know".

"See what you did? I was just illustrating my point".

"Yes, well, don't. I understood what you were talking about already".

"All right, sorry. Anyway, this energy can either come from the healer's own resources or it can be channelled from Spirit, or some say the Cosmos, and it is usually represented as a green or a blue light entering the healer through the head, from where it is channelled down to the hands and transferred to the affected area either on the healer personally or by the healer to the patient.

"What do you think of that, Becky?"

"I can't wait to read more next week".

"Yes, next week, I think we could try a bit of healing on each other. You could try my back and I will try to give you a general tonic. So, in order that you can keep up your studies, would you order us two copies of this book ASAP?"

"Yes, Dad, let's close now. I have to get home".

"All right, dear, I want to plant those herbs before it gets dark too. I'm sorry about your knuckles… I got a bit carried away".

By the time he had finished bedding the plants in, it was twighlight, but he wanted to water the garden before he went in for the night. He started in the front, and worked his way around, but when he beheld his back garden, he had to rub his eyes to believe them.

Kiddy and the Hounds of Annwn were lying on his lawn, looking for all the world as if they were taking a break mid-hunt.

A Night in Annwn

12. THE TRUMPET VOLUNTARY

William and Becky continued to make progress in their Development Circles and with their healing. There was not much visible advancement, but they had to learn to be able to concentrate at a higher level to do that. So, they continued to learn the theory and increase their power of concentration. William had a lot fewer obligations than Becky and so was able and willing to invest more time.

He also continued to receive encouragement and confirmation regarding his aptitude for listening, so when Sally arrived for her routine visit the following Monday morning, he tried to explain what had been happening to him after he had shown her around the garden.

"That is impressive for someone who has never done any gardening before, William".

"Oh, basically, I just took down the jungle that had overgrown Sarah's garden, and it was still there. It did look a bit shabby, but with regular watering and sunlight, it soon grew back", he explained modestly.

"What I really want to tell you about though, is that people from the Other World and this one have told me that I have an aptitude to listen. What do you think?"

Not knowing where he was coming from with this, she threw the question back at him. "What do you think about it, William?"

"Well I don't know, that is why I asked you".

"All right, but I am not sure what your question refers to. Please be more specific".

"Do you think that I am a good listener?"

"Yes, you are not prone to interrupting me when we talk. That is a sign of a good listener. Perhaps you like to listen to others speaking because you have spent so much time alone on the hill with your sheep. I don't know, that is only a guess".

"I think that you are right. In fact, I came to the same conclusion myself, shortly after I was first told the meaning of the silver trumpet. Er, I am not sure how to put this without sounding bigheaded, but people who should know what they are talking about... people whom I trust, say that I am making remarkable progress in certain fields, and I would like to put those skills to good use..." William discerned a brief look of alarm in his interlocutor's eyes. "I don't want to start teaching mysticism and Spiritualism. No, I am all too aware of my shortcomings in those departments, although perhaps I would have liked to try counselling, if the opportunity had been there for me twenty years ago.

"However, that is water under the bridge. What I am suggesting now is becoming a prison or hospital visitor, or both - a volunteer - someone who visits those who have no-one else to visit them. Now what do you think?"

"On the face of it it is an excellent idea".

"Why only on the face of it?"

"Simply because I know that such organizations exist, but I don't know whether they operate in this area. That's all. However, I could find out for you, if you want me to".

"Yes, I would appreciate that, Sally. I am sure that your office knows of these organisations".

"Yes, I am sure that you are right", she said making a note in her Filofax.

The following day, a woman from an office in Cardiff phoned him.

"Mr Jones? Jane Williams here. Sally Roberts gave me your number yesterday, Mr Jones. She says that you are interested in voluntary prison visitation. We need to have a talk. Can you come into our Cardiff office?"

"No, not really, I live in Bryn Teg, the Brecon Beacons and I don't have any transport".

"All right, we have a man who visits at home, I will ask Roger to phone you. Is that all right?"

"Yes, please do".

"On this number?"

"It's the only one I've got..."

"OK, thank you, Mr Jones".

An hour later, Roger phoned and at six o'clock he was at the cottage door.

"What a lovely cottage you have, Mr Jones. I would dearly like something such as this myself".

"Thank you, but Bill, please. Come on in".

They sat at the window table and Roger took out his laptop to take notes.

After an hour of questions and answers from both parties, Roger said. "Well, Bill, I don't mind telling you that I am satisfied. Of course, I have to pass my findings up to my boss who will make the final decision, but I am impressed by your manner and the way you live, so I don't foresee any problems. You will be expected to make the first visits with a supervised group, just so that there is someone there to advise you if you run into difficulties and we can recompense you for necessary out-of-pocket expenses, but we are a charity and money is tight.

"Other than that, I would like to say that it has been a pleasure meeting you, and I am sure we will again. Thanks for the tea and cake and your time".

After waving Roger off, William watered his gardens and reflected on the interview, for it was clear that that was what it was. He decided that it had gone well - the first job interview that he had ever had and at the age of sixty-five.

Three weeks later, he was sitting in Roger's car in the visitors' car park of Cardiff Prison.

"How are you feeling, Bill?"

"Pretty nervous, I suppose..."

"That is to be expected... I see it with every new visitor. Try to relax. Try not to see the inmate as a criminal, but just as a lonely man in need of a chat".

"I am all right, really. Let's go".

When the hour was up, Roger had to collect him from his booth.

"How did that go, Bill? You looked as if you had lost track of the time".

"Yes, I had. It was incredible he was the first convict or ex-con I have ever met - we don't get any on our hill, but I warmed to him and I think that he did to me as well. I feel sorry for the man. I didn't ask him what he was in for and he didn't tell me, but that didn't seem to matter. As you said, he was just a very lonely man in need of a good chat".

"I am glad that you enjoyed the experience. Most visitors find it rewarding".

"Yes, exactly, very rewarding".

Roger collected and returned William once a week for the first month, but then he had someone else to encourage, and it was not convenient to take him, so William caught the bus, and Roger collected his expenses claim for him.

One day, while sitting on the bus heading home, it occurred to him, that prior to joining the prison visiting charity, he had probably not been to the nation's capital more than once every ten years in his whole life, and now he was there every week. Brecon wasn't far from Cardiff, but he had had no reason to go there and his job had precluded frivolous visits anyway. Suddenly, he was beginning to feel quite the cosmopolitan.

After three months of travelling to Cardiff on the bus, he caught an earlier one one day and called into the office to meet Jane.

"It has occurred to me, Jane, that there must be many old and unemployed people in and around our village who would like to do the sort of work that I do. Perhaps not as often, but I don't know about that. If I could fill a minibus of, say twelve, would you pay for it?"

"If everyone was correctly vetted, and the cost was reasonable, I don't see why not in principle, William. Why? Would you be prepared to investigate such an addition to our team?"

"Yes, Jane, I would. I have gotten so much out of these visits, and I know that the inmates enjoy them, so I would love to try to push it further".

"OK, well, you make your enquiries and keep me informed, but only on the strictest understanding that I am not giving you the green light to recruit. You may carry out preliminary investigations, a feasibility study, if you like, and management will have a look at it. However, off the record, I think that it is a marvellous idea. Good luck with it".

William had never organized anything more than a sheep-dip in his life, but he gave his recruitment drive a lot of thought. It seemed to him that the first priority was to find out whether they would be able to hire a minibus, how many it would seat, and how much it would cost. Half a day, four hours, would cost fifty pounds, if the driver was allowed to freelance in his downtime in Cardiff. William had no idea about the costs of minibuses, but it put the cost of transporting twelve people at £4.20 each, which was less than he paid to get there on the bus, and the minibus would collect everyone from their home and take them back there. So, all he had to do next was fill up a bus.

William had no idea where to start except the place that he had visited most in the village, to wit the pub. He told Harry and Joyce his idea.

"The thing is, Harry", he said over a pint, "I get a lot out of my visits. I would actually say that I get more out of them than the prisoners. It gets me out of the house every week, and I get to wander around Cardiff for an hour all paid for. You know? I have seen more of our capital city in the last four months than in the rest of my sixty-five years put together! How many other people are there around here, who wouldn't mind a bit of that? I'm thinking of the old and unemployed for a kick-off".

"I don't know, Bill, but if you want to hang a poster on the notice board you can, and if you want to hold a meeting in the lounge one afternoon, you can have that free until six o'clock. No-one ever uses it in the afternoon during the week anyway".

"Well, thanks, Harry. You just pushed me further down the line than I was expecting to go, but I think that that is the way forward. So, now all I need is some flyers. Any preference for a day, Harry?"

"Make it a week Thursday".

It gave William ten days to prepare. Becky took her laptop to his house one evening and they designed a flyer which they were both proud of not being experts and she printed a dozen off at home.

William put one in the doctor's surgery, one in the village hall, one in the pub and one at the bus stop. The meeting was to be held at four o'clock, so that they could tap into the Thursday afternoon drinking crowd.

William took the chair of the meeting, another first for him, and he spoke to those who had come as friends, which they were. Everybody in the room had known everyone else for ever.

"There are four things that I can guarantee you: one that you will be helping someone whom you will end up empathising with; two you will enjoy the experience: three, you will get more out of the visit than the inmate and four, you will get a free trip to Cardiff every time you go".

Twenty-two people attended the meeting and sixteen registered an interest. William phoned the results through to Jane on Friday morning.

"That is incredible, William, you are a real powerhouse, aren't you? Let me put this to my superiors and I will get back to you as soon as I can. Thank you for all your effort".

However, William didn't feel as if he had expended any effort.

A month later, after Roger had had the chance to interview and vet the fifteen who stuck the selection procedure out to the end, his first busload of visitors left Bryn Teg in a joyous mood, as if they were on their way to a rugby match. It meant that three people could not go every visit, but they drew up a rota, which everyone was happy with, and sometimes people had to drop out at short notice, so all in all William's system worked out well.

After the first visit by the Bryn Teg group, William's standing in the community rose substantially, although sitting in his cottage or walking on Jones's Peak every day, he knew nothing about it. He would have preferred it that way too, if there had been a choice.

Six months after what Sally liked to call his near-death experience, William felt as if he was extending himself for the first time in his life. In short, he felt like a new man - empowered, and certainly more useful than ever before. He had always been a proud man, and usually with something to be proud of, but the feeling now was higher than that.

Instead of just being a proud working man, a proud upholder of the traditions of his family, he was now a proud helper of people, both imprisoned and free.

It raised him, although his reading had taught him the dangers of pride and he was on his guard against his ego.

The highlights of his month were no longer his visits to the Bethesda, but his visits to the Cardiff Prison, which, to him, seemed to help more people.

One night he made it a topic for meditation.

"I understand your point of view, William, but consider this", said John", you would never have started doing this, if it weren't for all the other experiences you have had and people you have met. When you collapsed, it was the catalyst that launched you down this path, but without the love and support of Sarah, you would not have met me yet. That was your turning point. However, to give you credit, you listened and took it further. Then, when you realized what was possible, you achieved this, but once again, you could never have done all this without the entities that you call Gareth, Emma, Mary, Sally, Roger and Jane, and not without the twelve to fifteen people who make up 'your team'. I am not trying to decry your input, William, I am just trying to say that it has been a team effort.

"In fact, every achievement is a team effort. Every single one of them. The history books teach children that Isambard Kingdom Brunel, built the Great Western Railway, but he did not. He conceived the idea and designed it, but none of it would have been possible without a supportive family, a team of technicians and thousands of workers. Similarly, pupils are taught that King So-And-So conquered somewhere.

"It is lazy history.

"Soldiers conquered those lands, and it has been ever thus. Nobody can do anything alone; everybody stands on the shoulders of others. The difference is that some admit it and others don't, and some have a vested interest in keeping the old myths alive, and others want the truth told.

"I think that you are one of the latter, William. Do not lose sight of the Truth".

"Thank you for keeping me focused, John". He did not believe that he had been egoistic over the recent events, but he knew enough to know that John knew everything about him, and perhaps more than he was willing to admit to himself.

He also realised that John had not mentioned any help from Annwn. John was obviously not looking for any credit, he was just trying to show his charge how to keep his feet firmly on the ground and his head out of the clouds.

However, it was still a fact that the lives of the visitors from Bryn Teg were enriched by their weekly visits to Cardiff Prison, and that transformed their outlook and behaviour. It had a beneficial effect on the community, making the village a happier, more unified place to live. The trips to Cardiff broadened their horizons, even though they usually only had an hour there to themselves. Many of the visitors liked to walk up from the prison to do shopping in Queen Street or St. Mary Street before catching the minibus back near the castle.

Bill and some of the men liked to have a pie and a pint in the Goat and Compasses near the castle

Many of the ladies did shopping for friends and family in the big chain stores which provided access to a wider choice and cheaper prices.

In short, the group of volunteers, who dubbed themselves Billy's Volunteers, much to his embarrassment, felt like a team and displayed the camaraderie of a yachting crew or an army platoon and other people liked to be in their company.

It didn't take long before Gareth heard of William's success with the volunteers and he discussed the matter with him one afternoon in his garden.

"This is a beautiful garden, William. The flowers in the front really light up the house and the road, and the smell from the herbs here in the back is exquisite".

"Thank you, you are most kind".

"Nonsense, it is one of the most well thought out and tranquil places I have been to for ages. There is a wonderful sense of love and caring here. It is truly a Garden of Eden."

"You will have me blushing in a minute. Another slice of bara brith?"

"Yes, please. Did you make it yourself?"

"Yes. Cooking is a new hobby of mine, but this is an old family recipe. My wife used to make it and so did my mother".

"You will have to let me have a copy, unless it is a family secret, of course. However, down to business. I have been hearing such good reports about your voluntary work at Cardiff Prison. I would like to know more. What gave you the idea, and how did you go about setting it up? With your permission, I would like to make notes and put your story on my little church blog and newsletter".

"Surely, no-one would be interested in that?"

"You would be surprised, William. It is a success story and people like success stories. There is far too much doom and gloom on the TV and in the newspapers. This is exactly the kind of thing that people like to read about".

William told his story from how it had all begun because Emma had told him that she had seen a silver trumpet hanging from his ear. They laughed when he explained that he had thought she was talking about a musical instrument, but Spirit, in the form of his Guide, John, and Emma herself had put him straight.

He told Gareth about all the support he had received from both sides of the grave, ranging from Harry's help with the venue to Becky's help with the printing. He did his best to give recognition to everyone who had played and was playing a rôle including the volunteers and the charity.

"That's marvellous, William. Just the sort of article I was looking for… and now I want to ask a favour of you, if I may?"

"Certainly, Gareth. Any time".

"I would like you to help me set up a hospital visiting service similar to your own. I realise that you may be too busy to run it, and it will be based in our village not your own, so transport would be awkward, but if you can help us get it up and running – point out any pitfalls, that sort of thing, Emma and I will take over the day to day admin.

"I have heard from friends what a positive effect your group, 'Billy's Volunteers', aren't you?, is having on the local community, and well, our village community spirit could do with uplifting as well and I think that you have hit on the way to do it without it costing anything. It will give the village its pride back".

"Yes, I'll help in any way that I can. The members of our group do seem better off for their visits. It has put a spring in their steps, and gives them something to look forward to every week – and something to talk about!"

"Excellent, William. You are truly an inspiration! I will go home now, write this up and get it published and we'll talk further in church. Draw up a list of everything you need, and anything you want me to do.

"Bye-bye for now and thanks for the interview and cake. I'll give you a ring later when the article is on line so you can check it for accuracy".

"Bye, Gareth", he said, but as he waved him off, he could hardly believe all the praise that Gareth had heaped upon him, because he still felt that he was getting more out of his activities than he was putting in.

13. THE LAST POST

When Gareth phoned to say that the article was live on the church blog, he thanked him and forwarded the URL to Becky so that she could check it for him, because he had never been on line, although he had a Smartphone with the capability.

"I'll have to get you to teach me how to use that Internet thing one day. In fact, why don't you order me a beginner's book?" he said to her before ringing off. William did a lot more reading now than he had ever done before, even when he was in school, and often regretted all the time he had wasted. He had spent decades of man-hours staring into the distance on the hill when he could have been educating himself... not necessarily in order to get a better job, he had enjoyed his life, but so that he had more to think about.

He now had eleven books in a row on his mantelpiece, and he had bought ten of them in the twelve months since his heart attack. The eleventh, The Holy Bible, had been handed down to him by his father. He enjoyed reading now, and did most of it in his back garden.

Becky phoned back to say that the piece was well written and accurate, as far as she knew, so William rang Gareth to tell him the same. He looked at the expensive piece of plastic in his hand and weighed it up. It was no more than six or seven ounces, yet it had just allowed three people, who lived miles apart, to collaborate on a piece of work, which would soon be visible to about half the world's population of seven billion Souls. It was mind-boggling to him on two levels. Firstly, the technology went clean over his head, but why had he ignored it for so long? Why had he sought reasons not to take part in a revolution, which was enabling mankind?

He did not understand what had made him so anti-progress. Was it having been a shepherd? After all, he could make his living with nothing but the clothes he stood up in and a stick, and he had often wondered why he had needed that as well. If that was his only excuse, it seemed very thin to him now.

Sixty-five years of looking backwards, not forwards! And how much time did he have now to make amends? No-one knew, and if they did they weren't saying. He guessed ten years.

When the first drops of evening rain fell, which had been predicted, he took his book and mug inside to his armchair.

"Do not be so hard on yourself, my love". He looked over the top of his book, saw Sarah and put it down. He rarely saw her outside because of the light, but conditions seemed perfect inside in the evening.

"It does no good to look back, unless it is to learn from one's mistakes. Doing it just to punish yourself serves no purpose".

"Hello, dearest, it just seems to me sometimes that I have wasted so much of my life".

"I don't think that that is true, but even if it were, you have an infinite number more lives to pick up the thread. You seem to forget that no-one is born with knowledge. A baby has one mental and one physical instinct: to show love to the person who feeds it, and to suck. All the rest is acquired. Everyone has lived before, so their Self has a repository of knowledge gleaned from previous lives, but not everyone knows how to tap into that source. However, if you learn how to do it in this life, it will be easier to remember how to do it in the next. Never take any notice of someone who confuses ignorance with stupidity, because they are only displaying their own stupidity, intolerance and prejudice. You know things that not all others know, and vice-versa, and so it must be and always will be.

"One lifetime is simply not long enough to learn everything. Take your time, learn at your own pace and be content with that, William. There is no-one looking over your shoulder tutting at you... Everyone here is pleased to see every tiny increase in someone's knowledge. Don't pay any attention to the professional critics, they don't know any more than you do, or they wouldn't be here.

"Before I leave you to prepare your tea, think of this. Who else, ever, throughout the whole of history in this area, has organised an event that keeps twenty-five people very happy every single week? And those twenty-five people infect the people they meet and live with with their happiness and enthusiasm. Other people may be able to speak foreign languages or use computers, but have they achieved that? You stick to your own past, Willy, you are doing well and we are proud of you".

William was on the verge of tears. He was not used to compliments, neither from his mother and father nor Sarah when she was on the Surface. It just wasn't the way of the folks in their area.

∞

William was enjoying helping Gareth set up his volunteer group. He was discovering an ability as an organiser that he had never suspected that he had and there were other surprises in store for him too. One morning Roger phoned to ask if he could call in.

"It's like this, William", he said accepting a cup and saucer and a slice of cake, "Jane and I feel that you have the skills and experience necessary to select your own team from now on. You don't need me to vet your visitors any longer. You know everyone around here far better than I ever will anyway. What do you say?"

"I say that I think that I can do that", he replied licking his teeth. "I have grown up with all the people around here, or they with me, but what about transport? Won't I need to go to their homes for the interview, like you came here?"

"No, not necessarily. I wanted to see how you lived, because I knew nothing about you. That is not the case with you and the local community. You could tell them to come here, or interview the candidates once a month in the village hall, or wherever you like. This would become your patch, but you could phone me or Jane for advice at any time. If you agree, I'll give you a wad of interview forms to use. You're not on the Internet, are you? No, well that doesn't matter. You fill in a form for each applicant, write 'approved' or 'not approved' at the bottom of each one, and send it in to Jane. She will accept your recommendation and inform the applicant accordingly. That way there is no come-back on you".

"Yes, I'll do it".

"Great! I was hoping you would, that frees me up to do other things. OK, well, I'll be off. Welcome to management, Bill". They shook hands and Roger left a flabbergasted William standing at his front gate.

A week later, Becky arrived unexpectedly in the back garden where he was reading.

"Hello, my dear. Nice to see you. To what do I owe this unexpected pleasure?"

"I did try to phone, but it's switched off..."

"It's charging in my room, but you don't have to ring ahead. I'll get you a cup of tea and a slice of cake". When he returned two minutes later, Becky said.

"Tea and bara brith on the lawn has become your trademark, Dad".

"How do you mean, Becky?" She passed him the local paper.

"Gareth said in his article how he interviewed you on the lawn with tea and homemade bara brith, and the local paper picked up on the article and copied it. People all over the county will be reading about you right now and all this week. Isn't it wonderful? You're a celebrity, Da!"

"Oh, come now... hardly. Only about thirty people read the local paper".

"Don't you believe it! I think it's closer to thirty thousand, and most of those papers are read by more than one person... next week, the free newspapers will pick it up. You mark my words, and they are put through every letterbox in the county. It's a nice photo too. You look like a country vicar without his dog collar. Did Gareth take that?"

"Yes. It is a good one of me, even if I do say so myself".

"Yes, well, I bought ten copies myself, so you can hang onto that one... and here is that book on the Internet you asked me to get for you".

"Oh, thanks, dear. How much do I owe you?"

"You are a celebrity this week and they get everything free, don't they?"

"No..."

"Yes, it is my pleasure. I am glad to see you taking an interest. Anyway, I only popped in to give you those things, give you a kiss, and say congratulations! The kids will be home soon, so I had better be going".

William saw his daughter off, sat down again, re-read the article twice and phoned Gareth.

Becky proved to be right about the free newspapers, but even she had not foreseen what also happened that week. A reporter from the South Wales Echo phoned one afternoon for an interview and arrived at William's cottage with a photographer. They said that they had read Gareth's piece in the local paper and their researchers had seen it on line, so they wanted to tell William's story from the personal angle. He gave them their interview, answered their questions and posed for their photos, but was bewildered when the reporters asked for some of his famous bara brith.

"I have some in the tin, of course, but I thought you being Cardiff boys would prefer tea and fruit cake. I'll get you some now. Just a sec".

"I will admit that it is not part of my regular diet, but I can't come up here and not sample your world-renowned bara brith. It would be like going to Thailand and not trying a curry. It would be unimaginable!"

"World-renowned? Come on, boys! Less of the flannel..."

"You take a look on the Internet. An interesting story can propagate around the world in hours, and yours has... In fact, I would place a small bet that someone will ask you for your recipe before long and my advice is to sell it, don't just give it to someone else to make a bundle from. It is delicious... it deserves to reach a wider public.

"Anyway, we have all we want, don't we, Rupert? So, we had better be making tracks".

"I would like a shot of William on the top of his hill where he used to work".

"Oh, yes, of course. Is that OK with you, William?"

They drove him to the top of the hill, took umpteen photographs of him with his staff, and dropped him off on the way back down.

No sooner had he phoned Becky with the news, than a researcher from S4C, the Welsh-language TV channel was on the phone to arrange an interview. They said that it was their intention to syndicate the footage to other broadcasters both British and worldwide. They said that it would probably be taken up in at least the United States, Canada, Australia and New Zealand. The interview was scheduled for the next day.

One of the interviewers seemed disappointed that he didn't have any sheep any longer, and asked if he could borrow one, but William drew the line at that.

"It's getting out of hand", he said to Becky the following Thursday morning on the phone. I haven't done anything to deserve all this attention".

"I know that you don't think so, Da, but other people think that you have. You are a local hero. The prisoners think the world of you and your team as well. I don't know whether you know it, but you have featured in the prison newsletter at least twice; and the mayor…"

She hesitated and William waited.

"Go on, what about the mayor?"

"No, I shouldn't have said that. It is supposed to be a surprise. Drat! Me and my big mouth…"

"Well, I won't ask you to betray a secret, but I am glad that I know that there is more to come…. As you know, I am not one for surprises".

William finished his housework, had his lunch, put his new 'Teach Yourself The Internet' handbook in his pocket and walked down to the village. Now that he was the area co-ordinator, he had to change all the posters to reflect his own contact details instead of Roger's. Becky had given him a memory stick with the updated file the night before, so he was hoping that Harry would print a few copies off for him to hang in the library, the village hall and his own pub.

Harry was more than willing to oblige and printed off five copies from his office equipment.

"If any of the boys come in, Harry, tell them I'll be back in an hour or so. I've only got to hang these flyers up and I'll be back".

"Righty-O, Bill. Congratulations on all that publicity by the way. You can't look anywhere these days, it seems, without seeing a story about you".

"Yes, thanks… I think, but none of it was my idea. I would rather have not had all the fuss, if it had been up to me. Anyway, I'll be back later".

He hung one of his flyers in the village hall and chatted with the caretaker, one of 'his' volunteers for a few minutes, and then proceeded to the small village library. He was surprised to see a desk with a computer on it by the volunteer librarian's counter

"This is new, isn't it?"

"Yes, Dai Evans donated it last week. Apparently he bought his daughter a new one for her birthday, so he gave us this one. You can use it if you like. It's free".

"Is it connected to the Internet?"

"Oh, yes. It is part of the village council's local area network. WiFi, you know?"

He did as it happened. That had been in chapter two of his book.

"All right then, I've never used one of these contraptions before, but I am in the process of learning how". He pulled the book out of his pocket and held it up.

"Let me see…" she said with professional interest. "Oh, I don't know that one. Any good, is it?"

"I'll let you know in a minute, if you'll give it back, Julie. I don't even know how to turn the thing on without it".

"Oh, I can help you there, William. Look, it is quiet now, so why don't I give you your first lesson?"

"How could a man refuse such an offer from one so fair as you, Julie? I'd be beholding to you".

Two hours and a lot of fun later, a customer entered the library causing William to check the time. He left Julie to her work and hurried back to the pub.

"Thanks, Harry. Lovely pint as always. That Julie Harris in the library was showing me how to use their new computer and two hours flew past in the twinkling of an eye".

"Ahhh, was it the Internet or Julie that distracted you, you old dog?"

"Please, Harry, I did not come here for abuse" he said with mock distain.

"Where do you normally go then, Bill?" said one of the customers causing a ripple of laughter.

"I shall ignore that remark", he said sipping his beer, "but I will say one thing. I wish I had discovered that there Internet years ago".

"Aye, Bill, there is no doubt bout it; the Internet is a powerful force. Many people prefer it to the telly these days, especially the young; but us oldies are catching on fast too", said Harry.

"Well, I might be a bit behind most, but I've caught the scent now and I'll soon catch up. I've got my book", he said taking it out f his pocket and handing it to Harry, "so there's no stopping me now"

"I can't fault you, Bill. Better late than never, is what they says, isn't it? I'll get the cards, shall I? Your oppo's just come in".

William didn't need to look around to know who it was. "Yes, and get the old duffer a pint as well… and a fresh one for me".

"How are you doing, me ol' mate? I've just been using your daughter's old computer in the library. That was vey kind of you".

"I wondered why you got me a pint without my having to twist your arm. Did you learn anything, or did you come out by the same door as in you went?"

"I did, as it happens, the front one, but if you are trying, in that subtle sledgehammer-like way of yours to ask whether I learned anything, yes I did, thank you very much. It was a profitable couple of hours, all made possible by the generosity of the kind lady librarian and your good self… which is why you are supping that free pint".

"Well, that's all right then, i'n' it? Glad to be of service… educating the ill-informed".

"I'll have you know that I was not ill-informed, I was just uninformed… but thank you all the same. How's the missus, Dai?"

"Ah, Ada's all right, thank you, Bill, just that she gets a touch of the old lumbago from time to time. And your Becky?"

"Yeah, yeah, she's all right thanks. Cut for deal…"

"Don't call me that, it's not nice!"

"Same old jokes.."

"The old ones are the best. King".

"Your deal".

Three hours and four pints later, William had had enough and wanted to go home. "I've had a lovely afternoon", he told his friends, "but I have learned to know when enough is enough, so I'm off for my tea. I'll see you all soon".

"Billy", said Harry, "you left your memory stick here earlier. Here it is. I hope you don't mind, but I put a load of military brass band stuff on there… I know you like Eddie Calvert and all the military tattoos. There's a young girl, er, Melissa Venema, playing Il Silenzio as well. It's magic."

Thanks, Harry. I'll listen to that when I get home, if I can find out how to".

"How are you getting home, Bill?"

"What do you mean? Walking, the same as always".

"I don't like the sound of that, do you, Dai?"

"What are you implying, sirs? Are you trying to say that I am incapable?"

"No, it's not that, Billy boy", said Dai, "but you know what happened last time you had one too many in the afternoon".

"Yes, Dai. A good point. Let me call Joyce down, and I'll give you a lift home, Bill".

"Please, I don't want any fuss, I can get home…"

"Yes, I'm sure you can, Bill" said Harry, "but for our peace of mind, I would rather take you… and I can show you how to access the music on that stick".

"All right, I know when I'm beat. Thank you, my friends. When do you want to go, Harry?"

"As soon as you are ready. You've got time for another, if you like".

"Yes, OK, and another for Dai, please".

Forty-five minutes later, Harry was in William's cottage showing him how to plug the memory stick into the MP3 socket of his music centre.

"Thanks, Harry. I didn't even know that that socket was there. So, I can download music from the Internet and play it through this?"

"Yes. It's easy. Anytime you want me to record some music for you, just let me know… As long as it isn't rap. I can't stand that stuff".

"Don't worry about it. I don't even know what it is. Brass bands, and brass instruments will do me. I'm looking forward to what you have put on here for me".

"Well, you just select MP3 instead of Radio, and click Play like so and off you go… Yes, there you go, it is starting. Right, well, I'll be off. I hope you enjoy it. See you soon, Bill".

"Yes, thanks for everything, Harry", he turned the music up and showed Harry to his car.

It was almost dark, but William turned a few lights on and the music up again and went outside to water the garden starting, as he usually did, at the front. The sounds of Lillibullero were blaring out of the open doors, but the nearest neighbours, four hundred yards away, would not be worried about that.

He cried when he heard Melissa Venema play Il Silenzio, and had to sit down to listen to it properly. If he had known how to replay that track he would have.

The last task that William wanted to perform that evening before making something to eat was tidy Kiddy's burial place. When Il Silenzio was over, he wiped his eyes with the back of his hand, called himself an old fool, and knelt at Kiddy's patch

"How are you, my old friend?" he asked quietly and she appeared before him. "I know that I can't stroke you, but I wish that I could. I miss you and Sarah so much…"

He wished that there were weeds that he could pull out, but he had tended it too well for that. As he sat on his knees, a pain like wind started, but it moved to his right arm and then to his chest.

He recognised the symptom.

'Marche des Parachutistes Belges' was playing, one of his favourite marches, not that he had ever been in a parachute regiment or any regiment at all. The pain increased but he didn't care. Sarah appeared before him.

"Come to me, my love, Willy. It is time to go home. You cannot fight this one and win".

He didn't need to be told twice, he fell forward into her outstretched arms. The brook between them disappeared and the band played on.

14. THE POST HORN GALLOP

As William accepted Sarah's embrace, the pain in his left side vanished. He cuddled up to her and stroked Kiddy's muzzle. "I feel as if this is how it should be" he said quickly.

"It can be however long you want it to be, my darling. You are in your natural element again now".

"Yes, it feels like it too. So what happens next?"

"Anything you want. You can have or do anything that you want, except influence the lives of the Surface-dwellers. They must make those changes for themselves... For example, you cannot stop them fighting, lying or cheating... they are there to learn how to do that themselves, just as we were... many times. These are difficult lessons to learn. The instinct to look after number one is born in us, it is why babies look at their parents so, and parents interpret that as love. It is not true love; it is a subterfuge to obtain more food. Some people continue to lie, cheat and steal all their lives, others don't.

"So, like I said, what happens now?"

"As I said, anything you like. However, judging by your recent desire for progress, you might want to get on with the next stage".

"Yes, which is?"

"You could call it 'Reassessment'. Before anyone returning from the Surface is allowed to take part in any further development, he or she has to review their most recent life".

"... and?"

"And nothing. You will be your most severe critic. You will know what you are ashamed of and what you are happy about. However, your reactions will be entirely up to you. Karma has already plotted your rewards and punishments for your actions".

"Well, I can't think of any regrets at the moment, can we do that tomorrow?"

"Yes, but there is no tomorrow here, there is only now... Remember the Roundheads in the pub?"

"Yes, well, let's just count to a hundred then, I am enjoying feeling your arms around me again".

She hugged him close. "I am so glad that you are home again, Willy".

"All right, I don't know how long I have been here, although it can't be long because my body is still lying there, but I do want to get on. How do I progress from here?"

"We, or you, I should say, can do it from here, but I always think that it is better done in the University. You know where it is, so just think".

They both put their sandals in a box, washed their feet, and walked up the steps. This time William found a door closer to the bottom. He tapped the door and looked at Sarah.

"No, I am afraid that this is something that you have to do alone. It can be a very painful experience. I will wait for you here".

"But I don't know how long I will be?"

"Time doesn't matter".

"All right, well I won't be long. I never abused Becky and I never cheated on you... see you shortly".

William's life was replayed to him in the same way that they say a dying man's life flashes before him. He saw clearly the pain that he had caused people over the years by silly or spiteful remarks. He saw how what he thought of as his natural reticence had caused Becky and Sarah to doubt that he loved them and he was tearfully sorry. When he left the classroom, he was still crying.

"I had no idea", he sobbed in her arms.

"I know, my dear. It is a heartbreaking experience for all of us... The pity of it all is that we see that, and go back to the Surface and do it again. Some do it less often every time, others never learn. Or that is not true, others take longer to learn... like the men in the pub. They will snap out of the loop they are in one day, but... well, that is up to them. It is their Karma".

"But I saw people crying over something I had said but they misinterpreted!"

"Yes, it can happen like that, which is why you have to be judicious with your choice of words. The Remembrance in the Akashic Hall is a humbling experience, but we have all been through it... and many times".

"How long was I in there, Sarah?"

"Er, as long as it took..."

"I see... this is going to take some getting used to, isn't it?"

"Yes, but not too long - because there is no such concept here... that is a Surface thing".

"Will you tell Becky about me, like you did last time?"

"I could do, but last time was not your time to pass over. This time was. We could do it together, if you like".

"Yes, I would like that. How?"

"Think yourself into her mind and say that you have passed on. She won't believe you, but you have to persuade her... or not, it doesn't matter".

"Let's give it a try".

Becky phoned her father and when there was no response, she drove to his house and found him crumpled over Kiddy's grave.

"Oh, Dad", she sobbed, but she couldn't think of a reason to be tearful except for the fact that she would miss his hugs.

"See that?" asked Sarah. "A beautiful moment..."

"Yes, she is a good girl... She has always cared. Will I be able to do anything about the funeral?"

"No, not unless you have done it already. You can try to make your presence felt though. There are usually one or two looking out for the deceased, as they say and I am sure that Becky will expect you to put in an appearance".

"Yes, well, I will do that, of course, if you let me know when it is".

∞

William was anxious to continue his education, so Sarah took him to the University again, and he chose a door.

"I have worked with animals all my life", he said to the woman who opened the door, so I would like to continue doing so for as long as I am needed".

"Come in, Brother", she said. "You are just the person we are looking for".

The work took William all around the Universe, because Earth was not the only planet where people kicked dogs and beat donkeys. It was a shock to him to realize how badly many people treated their animals. He was well aware that not all farm animals were pets, but they did all earn their keep. However, some people wanted more. He saw cruelty that made him cry many, many times. He couldn't understand why people would treat animals in such a fashion.

One 'day', Sarah told him that the day of his funeral had arrived. It seemed so irrelevant to him.

"You have to go really, William. I know that you think it's a bore, but some people will be hoping that you are there".

William looked at himself in the coffin, but he didn't think that the body did him justice. After all, the body in the box was that of an old man, and he looked twenty-five again now.

When the, his body was transferred to the church, he saw how many people had come to pay their last respects and it humbled him.

Every single able-bodied person in the village was there, as were the congregation of Gareth's church and a delegation from the prison on special release. He stood at the front with Sarah and John and watched. He was moved and surprised at the amount of genuine grief. He had expected Becky and her husband, John, to be there and their children, but he hadn't expected so much emotion from them.

Gareth and Emma saw him, Sarah and John and he was quite certain that other members of the congregation did as well. He made a point of trying to make himself visible to Becky, but he was just too inexperienced. However when he put an arm around her shoulder and whispered, "Don't cry, my dear, I am with your mother again", she turned to look at him and just said, "Dad?"

Several people spoke. Jane spoke of the first day she had met William and how she was impressed with his vitality. A prison warden talked about how much the inmates looked forward to the visits that William had organised and one of the prisoners told how William had saved him from committing suicide because he found prison life so dismal.

Gareth talked about the 'breath of fresh air' that William and Becky had brought to their congregation and how William had helped him establish a hospital visiting service and the owner of the taxi company told how William's custom had encouraged them to branch out into Cardiff.

Dai told of his life-long friendship with William and the mayor described how William's visitors, Billy's Volunteers, had improved the lives of so many villagers, which had, in turn, improved the lives of everyone in the area. He announced that the parish council had voted unanimously to place an oak bench in the park with a commemorative brass plaque in William's memory.

Finally, Becky gave a tearful, yet brave account of her life with and undying love for her father. When he put a hand on her shoulder and said, "Thank you, my dear", she looked at him again and announced that she thought that William was there with them. Emma nodded and pointed with a big smile.

At the crematorium, the vicar spoke of how William was a shining example of how one person, even in his latter years, could make such an impact on the community which had ripple effects as far away as the prison in Cardiff and the hospitals of Merthyr Tydfil and Abergavenny. William was truly moved by the outpouring of emotion and love towards him.

"I'm glad you persuaded me to come now, Sarah, though I do find it a little embarrassing".

"It is a part of the recovery process to learn what others think of us", she replied. "In your case, you have found out how much people, some of them strangers, were touched by your generosity, and returned your help with affection.

"Many others are not so pleased at what they see and hear at their funerals, I can tell you. Do you want to go to the wake? They are normally very enlightening".

"I think you ought to", said John.

"Will you both come with me?" he asked.

"Oh, you don't need me there. Sarah will take care of you, won't you?"

"Sure, forever and a day". William put his arm around her shoulder and she wrapped hers around his waist.

"Good, well, I'll be getting back then. I'll see you later. Have fun".

"Where are they having it?"

"Well, Becky did want to hold it in the cottage, but it was a bit too far our of the way, so she decided on her house. However, when Harry and Joyce heard about it, they offered the use of the pub, so it's being held there".

They willed themselves to the front bar of the Bryn Teg, but it was deserted. Everyone was still travelling back from the crematorium. They sat at a table and waited, like people had had to do in the old days before licensing hours were abolished. After a while they heard a key in the door and chattering voices. One of the coaches that Harry had laid on had arrived. Thirty-two people crowed around the bar thirsty for a drink, but no-one noticed them sitting there.

They had to laugh.

"I'm glad he had a good send off"; "You done 'im proud, 'Arry"; "I'm pleased that the weather stayed good for him. I always find it so sad when it rains at a funeral, don't you?" and "I could murder a pint" were typical expressions that they heard from the mourners

Within twenty minutes everyone was back and had been served.

"Order! Order!"

"A pint of Guinness, Harry, if you're buying!" laughed one man

"Very funny. Now, can I have a bit of hush, please?

"Becky and John have asked me to thank each and every one of you for showing your support this morning, and they want you to know, that there is a buffet in the back bar, which will be open in ten minutes when my dear lady wife has finished unwrapping the plates. And, they have put on a free bar until seven o'clock. So, ladies and gentlemen I ask you to raise your glasses to our friend William and express your gratitude to his daughter and son-in-law in the usual manner. God bless, William" he said raising his glass skywards. Then he put his glass on the bar and led the applause.

"Oh, one last thing before I forget. Becky tells me that it is likely that the last thing that William was listening to when he, er, at the moment of his demise, was a memory stick that I had just returned to him with recordings of his favourite music. Brass bands. Military bands, that sort of thing… So, I am going to be playing that music all afternoon, so don't any of you jokers go requesting anything else, because you won't be getting it and a refusal often causes offense".

No-one objected, many of them shared William's taste of music, especially those who had served in the forces, which William had not, although his father had done his two years national service in the Welsh Guards, which was probably where he got his love for it from, that and the Colliery Brass Bands that had proliferated in his youth, but which no longer existed. At least, the mines were closed although a few of the brass bands associated with them still struggled on.

"You know, Sarah, I am beginning to understand how those Roundheads can sit in a bar all day. This is fantastic! Great company, great music and a great atmosphere".

"This is your wake!"

"Are you trying to say that I or they should be sad?"

"No, my darling, I was just pointing out the irony. I don't believe that funerals or wakes should be sad. Far from it"

"I thought so. It doesn't look like there's going to be any weeping or a-wailing at my wake anyway. In a couple of hours, they won't remember what they're doing here".

"That's why mourners wear black – to remind them when they are drunk!" They both laughed and noticed Gareth and Emma watching them from across the room. They held up their drinks to them and William waved back.

"That reminds me of something that I have been wondering about for a while, Sarah. Do I now celebrate my leaving Annwn and being reborn on the Surface or my passing over from life on the Surface and my rebirth in Annwn?"

"Neither of them matter… "You can celebrate whatever days you like. The real thing is which birthday on Earth would you celebrate? The last one? The one before that? Every tenth one… or every hundredth?"

"Well, I can't remember any of the others?"

"I doubt if you can remember the last one, but you could research them all, if you wanted to. They are all in the Akashic Record and you can consult that whenever you like. The point is though, what is the point? Why would you want to know or care? What good will it do you or anyone else? It is just clutter. It is far better to occupy yourself with something that actually makes a difference. Like you have been doing this last year – or however long it has been".

"Yes, I see your point, my dear. Will I be able to work with you?"

"Yes, if you want to".

"I would like that very much".

"So, would I, my dear. I was hoping you would say that, because I have an idea that would draw our little family unit closer together, provide family entertainment and help others. Are you up for it?"

"I certainly am; tell me more".

"Well, Becky is going to miss you a lot, isn't she? You have always been a big part of her life, and especially so this last year, so why don't we channel ourselves through her?"

"A husband and wife double act?"

"And daughter – a family troupe. We would have to ask her, of course, but I think that she will like the idea. It would mean that we can all progress together, since she has never done any medium work and we have never channelled ourselves through one either".

"I think it's a marvellous idea. Perhaps Emma and Gareth could help her".

"Exactly what I was thinking, William!"

"We can add great minds to my list of 'greats' – great minds think alike. I can't wait to ask her… but how do we do that?"

"In her sleep. I do know how to do that much. Anyway, have you had enough here or do you want to stay a while longer?"

"No, I've had enough. I was hoping that one or two of the villagers might be able to see us, but it doesn't look like it. Let's just say 'Goodbye' to Becky".

"Good, because I have a surprise for you outside".

They passed through the crowd between them and her quite literally. Each put a hand on one of her shoulders and whispered 'Goodbye". She reacted and mouthed the words, 'Goodbye, Mum and Dad'. Those she was talking to ignored what she said embarrassed. Then they walked through the bar, through the buffet, through the wall and out into the car park at the rear. William heard the rear entrance open and turned.

"Oh, hello, Gareth and Emma. We were just leaving. It's not the same when you can't have a drink, is it?" he joked. "Thanks for coming". Sarah nudged him. "Oh, that reminds me. Sarah and I would like to channel through Becky, do you think you could help her from your end, and we, or Sarah, will do what she can from ours?"

"Yes, of course, we would love to help, wouldn't we, Emma?"

"Yes, it sounds exciting".

"Yes, I think it does too", agreed William. "Well, we will be in touch. Sarah has something planned for us. A surprise…"

"Yes, I think I know what it is", said Gareth looking over William's shoulder.

There were two jet-black Welsh cobs gazing at them, surrounded by the Hounds of Annwn.

"But, Sarah" William protested, "I have never been on a horse in my life!"

"Don't worry about it, you can't fall off… nothing can hurt anything in Annwn, and you can't keep up with hounds on foot can you? Mount up and stop whingeing. Think yourself into the saddle".

"I don't understand", he said looking at Gareth and Emma grinning. "If nothing can hurt anything in Annwn, what are we going to be hunting?"

"The wind, my dear. We are going to be chasing the wind! Tally-ho!" As the sound of the Post Horn Gallop came out of the pub, Sarah slapped the behind of William's cob and they raced off, closely followed by the Hounds of Annwn baying loudly.

Glossary

Bryn: hill
Coupy: squat
Kiddy: from *ci du* – Welsh for black dog (cŵn=dogs).
Teg: fair
Twp: crazy, mad
Y Tywyth Teg: The Fair Family; The Fair People; the Fairies

156

Bonus!
First chapter of the sequel:

LIFE IN ANNWN

The Story of Willy Jones's Afterlife

by

Owen Jones

1. THE FIRST DAY BACK

"Whoo-hoo, Sarah! I haven't been on a horse since I was a kid, when Dad used to take me riding on Sunday afternoons after dinner! I'd forgotten how much fun it is. Which way is home, love?"

"All roads lead to home, Willy! It's so nice to see you enjoying yourself, my dear!" replied his wife laughing, her auburn hair flying back in the slipstream as they galloped along on their magnificent black??? steeds.

"So, over that way, is it?" he asked pointing forward to a spot between two mountains.

"Yes, sure..."

"I thought I recognised it. I've always had a good sense of direction... I've lived in these hills all my life... Same as you, my love, eh?"

"Race you!" she laughed non-committally, and urged her mount on. Willy laughed out loud as he hadn't for several decades and gave chase to the horse that had a slight lead on him.

"Tally Ho!" he shouted as he clenched his horse between his knees and rocked forward. "Tally Ho!" In seconds, he had caught up and he leaned over to shout to his wife, "I don't believe in hunting just for the sake of it, as you know, Sarah, but I wish that those hounds were with us now... The Hounds of Annwn, you called them, didn't you?"

"Yes, my dear, but they are with us. Look behind us". As he stretched around to look, he became aware of seven??? huge Irish wolf hounds??? lolloping along just yards behind them. "Wow!" he shouted, "I can't believe I didn't notice them before. This is fantastic! So exhilarating! I feel twenty years younger".

"And you look it too, Willy".

A while later, as they were entering the valley between the two mountains, Willy, leaned over again. "OK, Sarah! Let's call it a draw! We can't be far from home now, but I'm having such a great time that I don't want to go back just yet. Can we stop here and lie on the grass? We can have a chat and play with the dogs while the horses rest a while".

"Sure, we can. Pick a spot".

Willy pulled his mount up within yards, saying, "This'll do right here. The grass looks soft and green, and the view is spectacular". They both dismounted and the dogs swarmed around them. "I didn't realise how tiring riding is until we stopped. My back is starting to ache too..."

"Don't think about it, Willy. You'll be all right in a minute. Come and sit here beside me".

"Don't we have to tether the horses to something?"

"Not really, but we can, if you like... To a sapling? There's one behind you". Willy turned slowly, his hand on the small of his back.

"s' Funny! I didn't notice that when we rode up".

"Didn't you, dear? Don't worry about it".

Willy tied the reins loosely to the six-foot Rowan, and sat next to his wife. "That's better... much better. I haven't enjoyed myself so much in years. It's great to be with you so much again. I have missed you, you know, since you passed away, or whatever you call it here. I forget now".

"I know, my dear, I know, but I never did leave you, you know. Not really. I was always there".

"But I couldn't see you or touch you".

"Granted, you couldn't touch me, but you could see me sometimes, couldn't you? And you did talk to me... quite often".

"Yes, I suppose I did, but you didn't reply".

"I like to think that you knew what I was saying".

"Yes, I think I did know, looking back on it".

"Yes, I'm sure you did. How is your back now?"

"My? Oh, yes, my back", he said rubbing it. "It's fine. No pain at all. It's just as if I had imagined it". Sarah smiled at him and continued to pet one of the hounds that was nuzzling into her arm.

"They really love you, don't they, those dogs?"

"Yes, and I really love them as well. I can't imagine why people called them the Hounds of Annwn, or Hell, in some cases. They wouldn't hurt a fly".

"Well, they are hunters, and they have to eat, so I suppose they have to do some er... I was going to say 'killing', but I suppose everything here is dead already, so... what do they eat? Talking about food, I'm getting rather peckish myself. I don't suppose you brought any of those sandwiches from my funeral, did you?"

Sarah was looking at him with a quizzical smile as she watched Willy trying to rationalise the situation he found himself in. "If you're hungry, my dear, you will find some sandwiches in my bag". Never liking to look in a lady's bag, even with permission, he put his hand inside and pulled out a large paper bag that felt right. "That's the one", she said. Willy took a few out and offered one to his wife.

"No, thank you, my dear, I rarely eat these days. You could say that I've got out of the habit".

Willy took a bite as she was talking, chewed and stared at her. "We don't need to eat any more, do we?"

"We can, if we want to, but it is not necessarily, no. Some people never realise that though and still eat like they did when they had a body to sustain".

"So, the dogs don't..." Sarah was shaking her head slowly and grinning, "either, so they don't hunt or kill anything..." He looked at the horses, "but the horses are eating the grass!"

"Only because you expect them to..."

"And my back? The same?"

Sarah nodded, smiling as if at a child who had just solved a logical problem. "And look at this", she said retrieving a mirror from her bag without looking.

"I really do look twenty years younger!" he exclaimed brushing his dark hair back with his hands. "And my hair has started growing again!"

"You said that you felt twenty years younger..."

"and so I look it..."

"Yes".

He stopped eating the sandwich and offered it to he nearest dog who took it and swallowed it whole. He looked at Sarah. "You wanted him to... you expected him to, so he did", she said with a shrug. "You can have what you want, as long as people or animals are willing to give it to you, but you can mould the scenery to whatever you want, because that doesn't hurt, can't hurt anyone, since we all see and hear what we want to without it affecting anyone else".

"Doesn't that make conversation rather difficult?"

"Has it with us?"

"No, come to think of it, it hasn't, has it?"

"Well, not for me, no... Nor for you, it seems. However, I choose to be on the same wavelength as you. You haven't really tried talking to anyone else yet, but some won't share with others, or won't try to communicate with people they don't know, but then that's up to them, isn't it? That's the world they choose to live in... some people like people and choose to help, and some don't, although that group is much smaller. Most people are basically nice... and helpful... in varying degrees, and the way forward is to become nicer and more helpful, if you want to put it that way... Onwards and Upwards!"

"I can see that I have lot to learn".

"Everyone has a lot to learn, don't worry about it. It is not a race, but most souls who arrive here need to be reminded about how life works, because the ways of the Surface have become imprinted upon them, but the impression does wear off, if you will allow it to, believe me..."

"It is going to take a bit of getting used to... I can see that... or does that mean that I am making problems for myself?"

"That is up to you. There's nothing wrong with being aware of a situation, but dwelling on it, or worrying about it can make it worse, or even probably will make it worse. There is no need to be paranoid about what you think, but it is definitely worth knowing that what you think exists and could affect you and your existence... even be it only temporarily..."

"The problem here is that in infinity, 'temporarily' could be a very long time... perhaps, thousands of years!"

"Yes, but that needn't be a problem... In infinity, thousands of years is less than a drop in the ocean, since there is a finite number of drops of water on any planet. What I am saying is that nothing can affect you adversely for ever except knowledge and that will always help, even though you, or one, may need to relearn, or remember, some lessons. Nothing can stop the steady improvement of the Self, even if some learn more quickly than others... As I said before, life is not a race or even a competition. And that is something that too many people have to learn, but there Ego's are so fragile that they have to feel superior to those around them.

"The true name of the game, to use an expression, is co-operation, not competition... Life is a team sport, if you like, not a solo event... Treating life like a solo event leads to loneliness, misery and selfishness, whereas if you treat it as a team event, it becomes a party! Or at least can do - that should be the goal".

"You make it all sound so lovely, my darling, Sarah, but then you always did have that knack. There isn't a bad bone in your body..."

She looked herself up and down and smiled, "There aren't any!"

"No, not now, but you know what I mean".

"Yes, thank you, Willy. You're not so bad yourself. You were a good husband and in difficult circumstances. I think we did our best for one another and our daughter".

"Whether it was our doing or hers, or a bit of both, our daughter has turned out all right. Anyway, enough of this Mutual Admiration Society meeting, I call it to a close. I'm not used to praise, I can't take it".

"No, I know what you mean... Getting a compliment out of a Welshman is like pulling teeth with chopsticks!"

"Was I that inattentive, Sarah dear? I didn't mean to be... another regret to add to the list..."

"It wasn't only you. It's just the way people were. We were all to busy getting on with a hard life. Don't worry about it, Willy, I know that I nagged you too sometimes".

"Not much, and I probably deserved it. At least I got to get out, and even go to the pub, but that cottage became your jail... and I knew it, but pretended that I didn't, because it suited me - I was selfish and I am so sorry for that now".

"Don't worry about it, Willy. It's all behind us now. You wouldn't be able to do that to me now though, even if you wanted to, although that doesn't mean that I wouldn't let it happen to me again in another incarnation. Life's funny like that".

"If you say so, my dear. Shall we move on now?"

"Sure, if you're ready. Where do you want to go?"

"I don't know... Home, I suppose".

"Home... All right. Do you want to live in town or on the mountain again?"

"Don't you already have somewhere you stay?"

"Er, well, er, it's difficult to explain..." She saw Willy's face reflect an inner turmoil and she guessed what the cause was. "No, it's not that. I haven't shacked up with anyone else - there are no nasty surprises in store for you! It's just that we don't need houses, just like we don't need bodies.

"Think about it. Why do people live in houses?"

"Well, er, it's normal, isn't it?"

"Yes, but they want shelter, privacy and security. However, we don't need to shelter from the weather because we have nothing to shelter and the weather is of our own making. We don't need privacy because we have no bodies, and anyway, if someone saw that you wanted to be alone, they would leave you alone - or most would... And security? We don't have anything that can be stolen..."

"Yes, I see".

"Having said that, lots of people still like to live in something somewhere. Life on the Surface seems to ingrain that very deeply into most people. So, what is it to be, within or without the city walls?"

"The city we were in before?"

"The City of Annwn? Yes, if you like".

"Won't it be hard to find somewhere at such short notice?"

"No, we'll just make the city a bit bigger, and put our house in there; or make a tower a bit taller and put our flat in or on it. Whatever you like. Or we could stay at the Inn while we think about it".

"Yes! I like that idea. We never did get much waiting on, did we? We only ever stayed in a hotel that week on our honeymoon in Rhyl. Yet when we first got married, I did so much want to give you a lady's life of luxury, Sarah. It just didn't work out like that... I'm sorry, my dear, so sorry". Tears flowed down his cheeks. Sarah shuffled over and put her arms around him.

"I know that now, and I knew that then. I knew what I was letting myself in for, and I did it willingly, because I loved, and still love you. You were always the dreamer, not me, Will Jones!"

"You were my rock, Sarah".

"And you mine"

"Come on, let's go and see if there's any room at the Inn".

Willy drew his head back to get a better look at his wife, "Now you're taking the Mick, aren't you?"

"Yes".

"Because there will be, won't there?"

"Yes. You're starting to get the hang of it".

"Will our old drinking mates be there?"

"They could be..."

"... if we want them to be".

"Yes", she said mounting up. "Come on then, Willy boy, race you again, see if you can win this time" and she sped off with the hounds all around her.

"Wait for me! That's not fair! I don't know where Annwn City is! I can't win!" He watched Sarah turn to face him. She was laughing out loud, looked in her twenties and was dressed like a maiden of the Fifteenth Century. He couldn't quite remember, but he was almost certain that she had been wearing her normal Twentieth Century gear a few moments before.

They rode and laughed for miles, or was it minutes? Willy could not be certain. It seemed that every time he tried to get a fix on time or a place, it moved. He was trying so hard to think in a linear pattern, but he couldn't. Every time he thought he had a fix on a concept, it seemed to squidge out between his grasp like jelly in a tight fist.

When he looked up from his contemplations, Sarah was rounding behind an outcrop??? of one of the two mountains and a fear of being alone in this strange land gripped him. He urged his horse on, and found himself at his wife's side. She had stopped to wait for him out of site, but before her was the huge, pinkish, front stone wall of Annwn City.

A flag, a pennant??? really, Willy thought, fluttered in the breeze atop a round tower within the walls.

"Wow! It's even more beautiful than I remember it", he murmured.

"Good", replied Sarah.

"I don't remember it being pink though".

"Don't you? Oh, well, we can change that..."

"No, I like it... it makes it look more like a comic book castle... no disrespect. More like Camelot in the cartoons, than Camelot..."

"Was there a Camelot?"

"I don't know, but if there were, I should imagine that it would have been more like Caerphilly Castle than that. I like it though, let's go in. Now I can race you to the gates!"

Willy arrived at the moat a length ahead of Sarah, but he knew in his mind that she had let him win. He looked up to the crenellated battlements above the drawbridge to see three men, who he supposed were guards, peering down at him. He turned rather sheepishly to Sarah.

"Guard! Squire William Jones and his wife, Sarah Jones, request entrance to the City of Annwn".

"Good day to you! Why do you make such a request unannounced?"

"We have travelled far and require shelter for a few days".

One guard disappeared, leaving the other two staring at the new arrivals. A minute later, the third man returned. "Your request for shelter has been granted. Please wait while we provide access" and with that chains could be heard clanking, which caused Willy's horse to rear up, and the drawbridge began to drop. When it was halfway down, they could see the portcullis being raised too. Willy grinned at Sarah, as if he were enjoying a role in a film.

When it was down, they trotted over the drawbridge and acknowledged the salutes from the guards inside. 'This way, my Lord", said Sarah light-heartedly and moved up in front. As they reined in their horses outside the inn they had visited before, the same landlord came running out to greet them.

"It is lovely to see you again, my Lord and Lady! I have the finest room anywhere in the city, if that is your requirement. Permit my lad to see to your horses. Boy! The horses, and look sharp about it!"

Willy and Sarah dismounted and followed the landlord inside. "It has been a lovely day, landlord", said Willy getting into the swing of things.

"That it has, my Lord. Indeed it has. Shall I have your things taken up to our finest room?"

Will looked to Sarah, unaware that they had any 'things' to take up.

"Yes, landlord. Please do that, but ask your boy to be careful with them. The caskets hold great sentimental value for us. They have been in my husband's family for generations". Willy looked at Sarah with an open mouth.

""Certainly, milady??? Please, take a seat, if that be hour pleasure. Oi! You lot! Keep the noise down or I'll stop your beer! We've got a real gentleman and his lady here now, and they don't want to have to listen to you rabble swearing!"

Willy looked behind him and noticed six men drinking at a table, who he presumed were the same ones as before. Sarah, only smiled at him and urged him by gesture to sit opposite her. "Do you want anything, dear?" she asked.

"I could murder a Ploughman's Lunch and a pint of bitter", he replied. "All that riding had made me right hungry and thirsty". Sarah peered briefly into his eyes, but it was enough to get her message across. She placed the order with their host.

"The riding didn't really make me hungry or thirsty, did it?"

"No", she smiled, "you did. You expected to feel hungry and thirsty... either that or it was he excuse that you might use because you wanted a pint and something to eat. Either way,it doesn't matter".

"Well, what was all that about our luggage? And what 'things'?"

"Oh, that? I was just indulging him, like I do with you. He was expecting us to have luggage, so I decided not to disappoint him. I didn't have to, but, well,it makes him feel better... in the same way that eating and drinking will make you feel better.

"Or to be more accurate, it won't... it will produce the empty satisfaction that buying something gives you. It lasts a few hours or a few days, but then you have to do it again. Like getting drunk every night... sooner or later, it is hoped, one will discover the complete futility of it and fix the cause for wanting to get drunk every night, so that you one can get on with one's real life".

"Which is?"

"Which is to learn, to acquire knowledge, and to put that knowledge to good use by helping others. Wisdom and altruism, in two concepts, if you like. If you have no knowledge, your desire to be helpful or altruistic might actually be harmful. You might do more harm than good... AND by doing good, you enhance your own Karma, thereby helping yourself!"

"Win win", he said, already convinced, but not wanting to hear the old mantra again. Hearing it still made him feel uncomfortable somewhere deep inside, even though he 'knew' it to be true. "Yes, I agree with you, but it doesn't trip off my tongue as easily as it does yours. I'm not ready to sound like a Hari Kishna yet".

"I know you're not, but you have already jumped the highest hurdles. You believe in it, and you live by it - more or less - but you are not yet prepared to come out and admit it to anyone but me".

He looked at her across the table, pursed his lips, then realised that he had done it, and so looked down at his hands. She had always been able to read him like a book, even before she had passed on. He was grateful when the landlady approached them with his food and drink. "Do you want anything, my dear?" he asked, immediately feeling foolish again.

Sarah grinned. "Yes, OK, I'll have a cheese sandwich and a glass of water to keep you company. Thank you". The landlady, a large jovial-looking fifty-odd-year-old in a rough dress and white apron, performed a slight curtsey, smiled broadly, and turned on her heel. "Won't be a jiffy, madam". She returned almost instantaneously and placed her wares before Sarah. "Enjoy your meal. Just shout if you need me. I'll be just behind that wall in the kitchen".

"You didn't have to do that just to please me, Sarah, but that you anyway. The strange thing is that I'm not really hungry any longer".

"That's not all that strange really. What would be strange is if you didn't want that pint either", she replied with a wicked grin.

"Oh, I can still find room for that", he laughed, playing along, but he realised that actually, he could take that or leave it as well. He took a mouthful and licked his lips. "Mmmm, Nectar???".

"Get away with you!" Willy looked down again, avoiding her gaze, and was surprised to see that Sarah's plate was empty bar a few crumbs. He looked up to see her watching him and smiled, she tilted her head to the side and smiled back. Everyone was happy - they had all gotten what they wanted. Willy took a bite of cheese and willed he rest away, but he was still surprised when it vanished before his very eyes.

Sarah clapped silently and mouthed 'well done'.

"OK, if we're not going to eat,and not going to drink... very much, what are we going to do? Do you want to go upstairs?"

"Willy Jones! What are you suggesting?" she said pretending to be affronted/offended.

"No, no! I didn't mean it like tha...", but he saw her laughing. "I suppose we are still married, aren't we? Do people, er... does that sort of thing go on here?"

"Yes, it still 'goes on', but we don't have any bodies and don't need to procreate. The thing is that not everyone realises that, so they carry on like they would have on the Surface. It's the same as drinking and eating. If you want to feel close to someone, there are other ways of doing it, which would have happened if you were making love to someone you loved on the Surface.

"We can talk about it again, if you like, but basically, it's more a melding or touching of souls rather than bodies... It's akin to the feeling you get when you meet someone and you like them immediately, or not, as the case may be. That feeling is produced by your non-physical bodies touching and being either in or out of harmony".

"Something else has been bothering me..." Sarah gave a slight upwards nod of encouragement. "Well, let's say that this was an inn with ten bedrooms, and it was full. Then you come along and turn it into an eleven-bedroomed inn, wouldn't the landlord notice? Or are they complicit?"

"No, not complicit, but he or and his wife might be aware of the change, although that is very seldom the case".

"Well, I don't get it then".

"No, it is difficult, but it has to do with parallel existences, worlds or Universes, whatever you want to call them. Here and now, this inn has always had eleven bedrooms, but in another existence, it, or one very much like it, may only have five. If this landlord woke up in the 'morning' and his hotel only had five rooms, he would probably think that he had gone mad.

"Having said that, there are people, or Souls, who know about parallel existences and can move freely between them, because they understand The Truth, and so are not locked in by their own beliefs. It's like the story about elephants..."

"Remind me..."

"Well, a mahout tethers a baby elephant to a deep stake so that it cannot escape. The baby elephant learns that trying to flee is futile and so stops trying. However, later, the elephant weighs two tons??? and could easily pull up that stake, but he doesn't try to, because he 'already knows' - he has already learned - that it is impossible.

"People do not believe in parallel existences, they are not taught about them on the Surface, or not widely, and so they cannot perceive them.

"If we left this, let's call it, eleven-bedroomed existence without paying our bill, this landlord would remember us for that, but the 'same' landlord in the five-bedroom existence would not know anything about it... or might know, or might have a vague feeling of 'irrational' distrust towards us. It is very difficult to tell how much people know without interacting with them.

"At least,it is for me. Someone more advanced than I might well be able to tell someone's level of attainment from their Aura. I am still learning about these things in school - for want of a better word".

"Yes, I see, said the blind man'. It's a lot to take in, isn't it?"

"Yes, it is, but that is the least of your worries... You, and everybody else, have all the time in the world to work it out. Come on, let's go to our room, and I'll show you what I meant by melding".

About the Author

Owen Jones, Amazon Best-Selling Author from Barry, Wales, has lived in several countries and travelled in many more. While studying Russian in the USSR in the '70's, he hobnobbed with spies on a regular basis; in Suriname, he got caught up in the 1982 coup; and while a company director, he joined the crew of four as the galley slave to sail, from Barry to Gibraltar, on a home-made concrete yacht, which was almost rammed by a Russian oil tanker and an American aircraft carrier. He now leads a somewhat quieter life in a remote village in northern Thailand.

As Owen puts it:
'Born in the Land of Song,
Living in the Land of Smiles'.

172

Other Books by the Same Author

Behind The Smile:

The Story of Lek, a Bar Girl in Pattaya
Daddy's Hobby
An Exciting Future
Maya – Illusion
The Lady in the Tree
Stepping Stones
The Dream
The Beginning

-

The Disallowed

Chupacabras on Backpacker Blood-Milkshake

-

Tiger Lily of Bangkok

When the Seeds of Revenge Blossom!

Tiger Lily of Bangkok in London

The Tiger Re-awakens!

-

Alien House

A Story of Love, Despair, and Alien Intervention!

-

Andropov's Cuckoo

A story of Love, Intrigue, and The KGB!

The Annwn – Heaven Series
A Night in Annwn
The Strange Story of Old Willy Jones' Near-Death Experience
Life in Annwn
The Story of Willy Jones' Life in Heaven
Leaving Annwn
Leaving Annwn on a Mission

-

Fate Twister
The Story of Wayne Gamm

-

Dead Centre
Not Every Suicide-Bomber Is Religious!
Dead Centre 2
Even The Wrong Can Be Right Sometimes!

-

Alien House
A Story of Love, Hope and Alien Intervention

-

Daisy's Chain
A Story of Love, Intrigue and The Underworld on The Costa del Sol

-

The Bull at the Gate
The Day the Sky Fell !

-

Owen Jones

The Psychic Megan Series
A Spirit Guide, A Ghost Tiger, and One Scary Mother!
The Misconception
Megan's Thirteenth
Megan's School Trip
Megan's School Exams
Megan's Followers
Megan and the Lost Cat
Megan and the Mayoress
Megan Faces Derision
Megan's Grandparents' Visit
Megan's Father Falls Ill
Megan Goes on Holiday
Megan and the Burglar
Megan and the Cyclist
Megan and the Old Lady
Megan's Garden
Megan Goes to the Zoo
Megan Goes Hiking
Megan and the W. I. Cookery Competition
Megan Goes Riding
Megan and the Radio One Beach Party
Megan Goes Yachting
Megan At Carnival
Megan's Christmas
Megan Catches Covid-19

Non-Fiction:

How to Give Your Dog a Real Dog's Life
and make him love you for it!

-

The Eternal Plan
— Revealed

(written by Colin Jones, compiled by Owen Jones)

-

How to Take Care of a Pet Rabbit
Cute Bunnies Make Excellent Pets!

-

Authorship
Publishing Your Book On You Own
http://owencerijones.com

For more information about my books and free audiobook copies,
please visit my blog at:
http://meganpublishingservices.com/

Review Request

Please write a review of this book, and the series, if you have read the trilogy, because your impression matters a lot to me and other readers. Don't underestimate the power of voicing your opinion.

Best wishes,
Owen Jones